La Luna

La Luna

A NOVEL BY

GEORGE MALKO

FROM THE SCREENPLAY BY

BERNARDO BERTOLUCCI

AND

GIUSEPPE BERTOLUCCI

PAN ORIGINAL

PAN BOOKS
LONDON AND SYDNEY

First published 1980 by Pan Books Ltd,
Cavaye Place, London SW10 9PG

ISBN 0 330 26084 7

Printed in Great Britain by
Richard Clay (The Chaucer Press) Ltd, Bungay, Suffolk

to the memory of JCS
who took me to Parma

PROLOGUE

The baby boy raised the small spoon and watched, fascinated, as honey began to dribble off it slowly. He moved the spoon and the honey made tracings on his naked leg. Pleased, he made a gurgling sound, and looked up. His mother, a young woman of about twenty named Catherine, stood near him on the veranda of the white one-storey house. Catherine had been looking out over the bright blue water of the Mediterranean, full of contentment and happiness. When she heard her baby she turned and looked down; she knelt next to him, and began to lick off the honey, cooing, 'Joey, Joey . . .' There was a piano playing somewhere from inside the house, but mother and son didn't seem to hear it. When Catherine reached for one of the baby's toys, he made to crawl over to get it. Catherine took him in her arms, and held him, feeling the sweet stickiness of the honey which was still on his small warm naked body. She could feel the rays of the setting sun, and closed her eyes, letting the baby's breathing mix with hers, feeling the light vivid pulse in her arms. She felt overwhelmed by love, and when she stood and held him in her arms there was a moment when mother and son were as the only two people alive on the face of the earth; their joy was special, and complete.

Catherine put the baby back down on the veranda and rolled a bright ball over to him. He gurgled once more. 'Joey,' she called to him, and crawled over to where he was sitting, resting his hands on the veranda's cooling stone surface.

A shadow suddenly fell across the child and he looked up, upset. It was his father, gigantic, towering over the tiny boy, the basket of freshly caught fish in his hands making him look even more enormous. He put down the basket and reached to pick up the boy, who was making for the safety of his mother. He lifted the naked child, tossed him up into the air and caught him. The baby made a small noise and his father tossed him up once more. It was several more moments before the baby was returned back to the safety of the ground.

He looked around for his mother, and couldn't find her. He made a noise, screwing up his face, and looked over to where his father sat, caught in the light of the sun. He sat on the veranda's low wall, cleaning and gutting the fish. His knife slit them neatly down the stomach, and then his large thumb dug down into the opening and slowly pushed out the pink and white insides.

Catherine, meantime, put on a record, a raucous 'twist' melody, and began to dance. She came out from inside the house, her body turning one way and then the other, moving towards where the man sat. The baby watched as he rose and joined her in the dance. The image, sharply outlined by the sun, was of two separate bodies coming together, joining in spasmodic movements, heads bobbing and weaving, lips wide in laughter which could not be heard over the loud dance music.

The baby struggled to its feet, and made for the house. He had caught himself up in the yarns of the knitting basket, and now dragged one of the yarns with him, leaving a long yellow trail behind him. When he came into the cool shadow of the house, he slowed, steadying himself against the door. The room before him was large, full of plump cushions and pale rugs. There were bamboo shades on the windows, and a feeling of quiet and calm. The boy moved forward and came to a mirror which stood leaning against a wall. He stopped and saw himself, a wondrous figure of another baby, right there in front of him. He reached out and made to grab it. He felt nothing, and tried again, and again touched nothing but cool glass. He gave up, reared back, and sat down. Rather than get back to his feet, he crawled further along the mirror until his image abruptly disappeared.

He continued and came to two bare feet, standing motionless. He stopped, pushed himself back and raised his head. A lovely woman in her forties smiled warmly down at him and then picked him up. She took him back to the piano where she had been sitting, and put him on the piano stool next to her. Then she began to play, improvising, humming to herself, inventing words. The rock music continued around them, but she ignored it, and played for the baby boy.

He looked around and saw his mother back out on the veranda, dancing. What he saw looked like a curious monster, four arms, four legs, and two laughing heads, moving in one body to the music. And then they stopped. The music continued, but out on the veranda the two figures no longer danced. They had become one, holding each other, swaying in a powerful embrace.

It was night, and the tiny boy sat in a baby-seat strapped to the handlebars of his mother's bicycle. He smiled up at her as she pedalled, but her face was wet with tears.

She rode along the shore, and the sea was suddenly visible, silver in the light of the moon. The baby gazed up at his mother, and beyond her saw the moon, large and yellow. As she pedalled and her position shifted, the child could see the moon moving, jumping from one side of her to the other. He did not realize his mother was weeping desperately, her sobs helpless. He wanted to get her attention and waggled a hand at her, gurling. He bobbed up and down and touched his diaper until she reached between his legs and felt for a moment. She looked closely at him, barely visible in the white pale light, and had to smile. The tears streamed down her face, but she looked at her son and smiled.

He returned her stare and was happy, but then he saw the moon again, there right next to his mother's face. There were two things to see above him, moving, swaying as the bicycle continued on its way: there was the very young face of his mother, and the ancient disc of the moon.

ONE

It was pure coincidence that Caterina was standing looking out of the window as Douglas's car turned the corner into Columbia Heights Avenue and headed towards the house. 'I'm going to take the car to the garage,' he had said. 'I'll be back in a few minutes.' Caterina was thirty-five years old now, and even in her dressing gown, a coffee cup in one hand, she held herself with what she knew was that acquired elegance of the performer, the soprano – Caterina Silveri, born Catherine Silver but now recognized, particularly in Italy where her career had originally flowered, thanks to Douglas's astute guidance, as an authentic opera star.

The three-storey house in Brooklyn Heights looked the way it always did when she and Douglas were preparing to leave for Europe: trunks everywhere, most of them still open, clothes in one, musical scores in another. Molly, the maid, was making desultory moves to clear the table of the breakfast dishes and Caterina turned her out, did that little trick of hers to avoid telling her to get a move on. Molly would be staying to take care of Joe and this was certainly not the moment to get shitty with her.

Joe was fourteen years old now, soon to be fifteen. Caterina was concerned about leaving him; she knew Joe resented being left. At breakfast, earlier, she'd been taking notes, going over her schedule, checking her diary, and had said to him, 'You know you have a dental appointment. Next Thursday, at three, to get your teeth cleaned.'

'Oh, yeah,' he had answered and bitten into a piece of toast.

'Don't forget,' she had added, and looked over at Douglas, who was finishing his coffee.

It seemed to Caterina, had always seemed to her, that she was the one who made sure everything was being organized;

Douglas was supposed to be the one who took care of details, but she was the one who finally had to check everything. 'Did we pack the Chinese dressing gown?' she had asked Molly as the maid came by with fresh coffee.

'It's in the silver trunk,' Molly had answered.

Caterina had nodded and got up, mentally going over all of the other things she wanted to be sure had been packed. She went into the music room and began to collect musical scores, crossing to put them into the large case in which they were always carried. '*Tutte le feste al tempio . . .*' she had begun to sing, partly to herself, going over it to help remember words she knew she sometimes forgot, and partly to practise. '*Every holiday at church . . .*' It was an aria from *Rigoletto*. Gilda sings it, fearfully recounting to her father, Rigoletto, how she was heartlessly carried off by courtiers led by the Count of Ceprano. It was a complicated plot, intertwined, full of mistaken identities and melodramatic unmaskings, but it was nothing without the music, Verdi's soaring music.

Molly had offered Douglas another cup of coffee and he had said his usual 'No, thanks,' which as always prompted her to give him something of a critical look. Douglas had risen and smiled down at her. He was very tall and distinguished looking, an impressive man in his early fifties who took good care of himself.

'Are you growing again?' Molly had asked him with a trace of a slow grin.

'Growing a little every day,' Douglas had said with mock gravity, and then went out to where Caterina was continuing to put away music scores. Joe had stayed where he was, chewing on a piece of toast and noisily swallowing orange juice.

'*. . . mentre pregava Iddio*,' Caterina had been singing as Douglas came in and went over to stand by the piano, out of her way as she went to and fro with things for the suitcases. He listened and watched her with unadorned admiration. Her voice was superb. '*. . . bello e fatale, un giovane offriarsi al guardo mio . . . Se il labbri nostri tacquero, dagl'occhi il cor, il cor parlo.*'

'Can I help?' Douglas had offered.

She'd given him a smile and a small shake of her head, and then began humming the melody to herself – in her mind she was saying the words, knowing their meaning – '. . . *as I was praying to God, a young man, handsome and irresistible, offered himself to my gaze . . . and though our lips were silent, our hearts spoke to each other through our eyes.*'

'I had a strange dream last night,' Douglas had said, which made her stop singing and turn to him.

'What?'

Seeing her expression, he'd shaken his head. 'Oh, it's, it's boring.'

'Tell me,' she'd urged.

'No, you're busy packing. I'll tell you later.'

'You always tell me your dreams,' she'd said.

Douglas had brushed this off, saying, 'When people tell me their dreams, I find it very uninteresting. I'll tell you later. We'll have time on the boat, okay?' He had started out of the room, heading for the stairs. 'Remember, we have to be ready in two hours.'

'So you'll bore me on the boat,' she'd said and laughed. It was a small joke between them, taking the boat when modern opera schedules were planned around everyone taking planes. But Caterina's trips were extended, always for a few months, and she insisted on bringing along what she would need, what she knew she could depend on. If she arrived at the dock looking like some pre-war *diva* about to board the Orient Express, so what? She was a star, and the reporters always gave her terrific coverage.

Joe had been watching, waiting, and when Douglas had gone upstairs he'd got up from the table and gone into the music room. Caterina had passed him once or twice, carrying musical scores, and then he'd said, 'You never take me with you.'

She had been singing '*Tutte le feste al tempio . . .*' again, from the beginning, and had stopped to look at him. 'It's not true,' she had said, 'you know that. I took you to Washington, I took you to Seattle . . .'

'I want to go to Italy with you,' Joe had insisted.

She had been saying, 'I took you to Boston, to Philadelphia . . .' and she was about to continue listing cities, but instead had stopped to face him and say, with a certain finality, 'I can't.'

'Why not?' Joe had said quickly. 'I can do all the things Dad does. I can make reservations for you – ' it was spilling out of him fast, ' – I can negotiate your contract for you.'

Caterina had given him an affectionate look and said, 'Come on.'

'I can,' he insisted.

'That's what Dad does.'

'Yes,' Joe had said with a trace of resentment, 'but I can do it better.'

'What about school?'

'Let me come,' he'd repeated, almost pleading.

'No.'

'Yes.'

'No,' Caterina had said with gentle firmness, and began to repeat it, her tone affectionate. 'No – no – no – no – no . . .'

'All right,' he'd surrendered. 'All right.'

She'd softened immediately, and said, 'Next time,' but Joe was out of the room and she heard him clumping up the stairs.

Douglas was in the study, sipping a drink. Joe had walked in, seen him with the glass in his hand, and stopped. 'Are you drinking?'

Douglas had turned, looked at Joe, and nodded. 'Yes, I am.' He took another small swallow, savoured it, and then used the glass to indiacte the television set. 'You know what I saw on cable last night? I saw a Chinese TV show. This little Chinaman comes out and starts to talk, in Chinese, and underneath him are subtitles, in Chinese.' Joe had grinned. Douglas had taken a sip and his expression grew thoughtful. 'Weird,' he had added.

Joe's eyes went to the drink and he asked, 'What is it?'

Douglas had stared at his glass and then at Joe. 'It's brandy. It's very good brandy, older than you are. Much older.' He had gone over to take an appreciative look at the brandy bottle and didn't see Joe's look. Douglas put the bottle away and stopped because he had seen something out on the terrace. He went over and opened the doors. 'What's my tennis racket doing out here?'

'I was trying to hit a ball into the river,' Joe had answered.

Douglas had stepped out on to the terrace and picked up the racket. Joe followed him. 'The river?' Douglas said and gave a small laugh. 'You want to see me hit the city?'

Joe's face lit up and he said, 'I'll bet you a buck you can't do it.' Douglas had given a small laugh and prepared to swing, winding up, when Joe interrupted him. 'Hey, Dad,' he said, 'why don't you stay here with me? You and I could have so much fun together. Mom doesn't need you. She can get somebody else to do all her junk for her. Come on. You and me can go to the ball park. We could have so much fun.'

Douglas had lowered the tennis racket and stared at Joe, and then smiled. 'That's a fine idea, Joe. We must do it.'

Joe wasn't sure he'd heard right. 'You mean it?'

'Absolutely,' Douglas had said, and then wound up, tossed the tennis ball up into the air, and swatted it with the racket. The ball had taken off, up, out over the parkway, and then dropped.

Joe grinned triumphantly and held out his hand. Douglas put the racket under his arm, shoved a hand into his pocket, and pulled out some bills. He found a single, and handed it to Joe, who pocketed it immediately.

Douglas took the racket out from under his arm and held it out to Joe. 'Could you take this down for me, put it into the blue suitcase?'

Joe had looked at Douglas, and then his expression fell. He took the racket and turned to walk angrily out of the room, throwing, 'I get it,' bitterly over his shoulder.

Douglas had come back in and retrieved his glass, and then turned and looked back out of the open doors, at Manhattan across the harbour. He stepped back out on to the terrace and took a long look at the distant skyscrapers, all of them pressed together so closely. He didn't notice that Caterina had appeared on the terrace below, a fresh cup of coffee in her hand. Douglas ran his hand slowly along the railing, and came across a big wad of bubble gum stuck there. He fingered it, his expression distasteful, and muttered, 'Jesus Christ, he leaves his gum all over the place.'

From below, Caterina had cocked her head, looked up and seen him. 'You talking to me?' she had called out.

Douglas had looked down at her and gave his head a shake. 'No,' he'd said. 'I was just talking to myself. I'm going to take the car down to the garage.' He turned to go back inside. 'I'll be back in a few minutes.' He'd said that, and disappeared into the house . . .

So now she watched his car coming towards the house, her mind wandering as it did so often: the trunks, Douglas's dream – another dream? – Joe, Joe desperate to go with her, '*un giovane offriasi* – ' and as she watched, the car slowed, its wheels turned to steer it into the wrong lane, and suddenly it speeded up, an abrupt jerk, a terrible jolt that pulled it into a sharp swerve, back in to its own lane, across it, up, on to the sidewalk, into garbage cans that scattered spilling garbage, stopping inches from a huge metal fence.

Caterina was down the stairs and out of the door, the coffee cup in her hand still, moving slowly, and then more quickly, hurrying across the street, blind to passing cars, slowing to stare at Douglas's car jammed across the roadway. People were already stopping to look inside – someone had jumped out of one car and was hammering on one of the doors, trying to get it open. Caterina got to the driver's side and yanked at the door but it was locked. She could see Douglas slumped over the wheel. He wasn't moving. 'Douglas . . .' she said once in a strangled voice, and could only stare.

Beyond her, Joe came out of the door, breaking into a run. He crossed the street, pushing past his mother, and grabbed the door and pulled on it. It wouldn't budge. He began to bang on the window, trying desperately to get the door open. It was hopeless. All he could do finally was lean his head helplessly against the door's window. 'Dead . . .' he moaned. 'Dead, dead

. . .' Douglas sat collapsed, his head resting on the steering wheel. His heart had stopped, for ever, struck suddenly by a massive coronary. 'Dead,' Joe cried more loudly. 'Dead, dead, dead . . .'

TWO

The water on the small pond was grey as the sky above it. Ducks and geese, Canadas and whites, flap-padded up out of the water and waddled around, milling uncertainly, wary of the gathering in the distance. Joe watched the birds, trying not to hear the minister's word. He was in a cemetery and knew he should feel something respectful and proper, but he was angry, he hated all those people gathered around the open grave, hated the way they respectfully deferred to him as he and his mother moved among them. Joe couldn't stand it, and had moved off, over to the pond.

He turned and started back towards the grave, plodding through old leaves, the plaintive honking fading behind him as the minister's words came to him more clearly – '. . . by his death.'

What the fuck does he know, Joe thought, and moved in among the people, pausing by Molly's side. The large black woman was sobbing loudly, dabbing at her eyes. 'Stop crying,' Joe said to her, and when she didn't respond he carefully put his foot on top of hers and slowly ground down. Her eyes widened and flicked over to stare at him, dumbfounded.

'We might be fully reconciled,' the minster was finishing, 'to this joy.'

'Would you please stop crying,' Joe said to Molly, staring at her.

'Amen,' the minister said, but Joe was already moving around the mourners, passing behind them even as Caterina tossed a white carnation on top of the coffin.

Caterina saw him as he moved away from Molly and followed him with her eyes. More flowers fell on to the coffin. She separated herself from the small crowd as some of them were moving away, towards the parked limousines. They were all in black, fur collars turned up against the raw cold. There were austere coats and severe capes and it was all grandly muted, the opera world, Douglas's friends, Caterina's devoted admirers. Joe was getting into the first car as she set out after him. People nodded to her, one or two reached out to her, but her step quickened and she ignored them. A feathered hat dipped to her, a gloved hand offered support, but she wanted only to get to the car and join her son.

He was waiting with his face pressed against the window, tears on his cheeks. He wouldn't look at her. She settled herself next to him, drying her eyes and then wiping her nose. 'I don't like these people,' she said with soft bitterness. 'I can't stand them.' She was dimly aware of shapes passing the car; someone bent over to peer inside.

'Are those ducks, or geese?' Joe asked.

Caterina didn't hear. 'I can't spend another night in the house, Joe,' she said. 'I can't. I can't do it. I want to leave on the next available flight.'

Joe turned and stared at her. 'What about me?'

Caterina looked at him, as if surprised he'd say something like that. 'Why, you'll come with me, darling. We'll spend the night on the plane.' Her urgency grew, mixed with the need to believe what she was saying. 'We'll sleep, we'll rest, we'll wake up . . . we'll be in Italy.'

'Italy!' Joe said, shocked.

'I'll go to rehearsal. I'll sing.' Caterina was making a list, going over the very solid and dependable foundations of her life. She was a professional and when she looked at Joe, her eyes red, she wiped them with a gloved hand and said, 'Darling, you can put your things in the dark trunk. You can put your music in with my music. And your records. And you can put your clothes—'

'I've got school,' Joe interrupted her.

'—with my clothes.' She stopped. 'School? Joe, there're schools in Rome. It's not a problem.'

'But I've got a big game coming up,' he said. 'It's important to me. I have to play. They can't play without me.'

'A game,' Caterina said uncertainly, wondering, why was he arguing with her? He'd wanted to go, begged her. Why was he arguing?

'You knew about it,' Joe said unhappily. 'You knew all about it.'

'Oh, Joe,' Caterina said with despair, 'you're making this very difficult. Joe, please. Help me, darling.' She reached for him and drew him close to her. Unable to control herself, she felt the tears coming. 'Help me. Help me.' She swallowed, holding her son tightly. 'Help me, please.'

Joe pressed against his mother. He felt something and looked up. Faces were peering in at all the windows, from both sides and from the back, curious, grossly solicitous faces, with looks of empty inquiry. 'Ma,' he whispered, frightened, 'please, let's get out of here.'

Now Caterina noticed them, saw the grey sheen of a hairdo and the pale pink of a woman's lips. She suppressed a gasp and forced herself to lean forward to talk to the driver. 'Could you drive us home?' she said. 'Please?'

'Yes, ma'am,' he said politely and started the engine.

The mourners parted silently as the big black car slowly drew away from them and drove off down the tree-lined roadway, past the bleak concrete monuments and even rows of headstones, away from the other limousines, away from the departing mourners, away from the pond and the ducks and geese who now moved more confidently across the path towards the grave where Douglas's coffin was silently descending into the damp ground.

THREE

It was three months later.

Joe had never played in the big game. They hadn't left the night of the funeral, but they might just as well have. Caterina was up all night, packing and repacking. She had supervised Joe as he collected the things she thought he would need and then had started to help him put them into the luggage. When she had come across the first of Douglas's things that would have to be taken out, she had uttered a strangled cry and rushed out of the room. Molly, who had been hovering on the periphery of all this, swallowing heavy sobs and clutching a wet handkerchief to her eyes, had rushed after her, leaving Joe with the open suitcase and a pair of Douglas's purple boxer shorts on the floor in front of him. He'd stared down at them, uncertain what he should be feeling, and then something had frightened him, a terrible feeling, unsettling, distant, and he'd kicked the shorts under the coffee table and slammed down the lid of the case.

They had finally got everything arranged, though Caterina kept moaning that nothing was organized, she never knew where anything was, it would take her for ever to remember where everything had been put. Worse, when she had tried to explain to Molly what had to be done with the house once she and Joe were gone, Molly had nodded as if she understood. The moment Caterina asked her to repeat what had been said, she collapsed in a torrent of helpless tears, wailing, 'Ah cain't, Mis' Silveri. Ah cain't!'

Caterina had been up all night by this time and had grabbed Molly by the shoulders to give her a good shake. 'Pull yourself together,' she ordered sternly. 'Damn it now, Molly, it's over and we don't need any more of it.'

'Yes, ma'am,' Molly had dutifully echoed, 'it's over.'

For Caterina, it was as if she had heard the words for the first time. She had paled, and she had felt giddy. 'Over . . .' she had said softly, and had to be helped to a chair.

Joe had kept to his room, almost hiding out there. Molly had brought him some lunch and had started to tell him how sorry she was but she had seen the look on his face and clammed up. Later, Caterina had appeared, to tell him they were booked on the nine o'clock flight to Rome. Non-stop.

'What about my stuff?' Joe had asked.

'That's being shipped,' Caterina had said. 'Molly will see to it.'

'She couldn't see shit!' Joe had spat.

'Joey!' Caterina had cried, knowing the uneasy antagonism that had always been there just below the surface between her son and their housekeeper. 'She's upset. You leave her alone.' She had started out of his room but had stopped to turn back to him one last time. 'God damn you,' she'd said bitterly, 'just leave her alone.' She'd seen the look on his face, the anger clouding it, and had realized she shouldn't have gone that far. She came over to him and put her arms around him and, even as she felt him resisting her grasp, she had held him to her. 'I'm sorry, baby,' she had whispered. 'I'm so sorry.'

The first few weeks in Rome had been a madhouse. They had stayed first in a hotel and then in a small furnished apartment that Caterina's old friend, a woman named Marina, had rented for them sight unseen. Caterina had taken one look at it and lost her temper. Joe had never seen his mother throw a real tantrum; he loved it. He didn't care why she was doing it, he just loved it. A week later, they were out of the place and for a few weeks Caterina's friendship with Marina was sort of cool because it had looked as if Marina would get stuck with the deposit she'd put down on the place. She hadn't, and had made a point of going with Caterina to look at all kinds of unfurnished apartments. Her devotion had been tireless, long after Joe had declared he didn't give a shit where they ended up living, just as long as he had his own room and didn't have to look out at a wall. One of his friends from Manhattan, a terrific kid named Lloyd, had a room the size of a closet and a window that looked out on a big blank wall. He and Joe had once had a pissing contest, out of Lloyd's window, to see who could cover the widest area of the wall. Joe had lost, even though he had managed to write the letter 'J'. 'That's what that fuckin' thing's good for!' Lloyd had declared.

Caterina had enrolled Joe in one of the international schools, and even though he'd resisted the idea, once he'd started going to classes he felt better. The place was more of a big villa than a school – it never felt like a school to Joe – and the teachers were pretty much a mess, with a couple of exceptions. They were either very young, just out of some American college or a European graduate school, or old and nervous. Joe thought of them as being dusty; there was one biddy who kept clapping herself on the shoulder like it was dusty. The classes were reasonably small and the work wasn't too hard, except for the languages, which Joe had told Caterina gave him the shits. She had only half heard him because her attention was taken up with her rehearsals by then. She had plunged back into work like some sort of maniac. When their trunks had finally arrived she and Marina had spent three days going through all the musical scores, arranging them in one of the rooms of the new unfurnished apartment. Joe had walked in on them one morning, his mother clutching a score to her breast, moaning tragically, 'I can't, I can't, I can't,' with Marina hovering nearby, touching her comfortingly, fluttering like some bird with two broken wings, repeating, 'It's all right, it's all right, it's all right.' She had seen Joe in the open doorway, watching, and had scurried over as Caterina continued to clutch the music score to her bosom. Marina had leaned close to Joe and had imparted the cryptic revelation, '*Trovatore*,' and then hurried back to resume comforting the prima donna.

A lot of Joe's schoolmates were driven to school in these big limousines. Most of them were Fiats and Bentleys and the biggest Mercedes Benz Joe had ever seen, complete with a bar, radio and television, and two telephones. There was one Cadillac, a custom job which brought a small Arab kid right to the school's door every morning; two bodyguards would leap out of the car and run around to the back door and open it for the kid who would peep out meekly and then let one of them take his hand and lead him into the school. The car would remain parked outside the school for the entire school day and one of the armed guards would attend every one of the kid's classes with him. When Joe had asked someone what was going on, the answer had been, 'The little creep's worth millions. Somebody tried to snatch him last year. The little creep's worth millions.'

The kids at the school were a little like the cars. They came from all over, and some of them didn't really fit in Rome. Joe felt a little like that, though he couldn't quite figure out what it was that sometimes nagged at him. Maybe it was everybody trying to act American when so many of them weren't. They had the swagger, when they cruised an avenue, and they had the look, the Levi's and the Adidas sneakers and the T-shirts with the iron-on pictures. But everybody in Europe wore that stuff now, there was no way of telling a European teenager from a kid from Chicago. So what was it these kids were trying to do when they came into an ice cream bar and acted as if they were taking over the place? Joe couldn't figure out what they were trying to prove. The ones who were least American, like the kids of one of the Spanish diplomats posted to the Vatican, they came on like a couple of hip dudes One of them had come on strong with Joe until Joe had said, 'You know, you're really a jive turkey,' which had blown the kid away and from then on, again for some weird reason, the kid had treated Joe with new respect. Joe had seen it back home; it was because Joe was legitimately American. But why it mattered at all, he couldn't figure out. If all these kids living in this faraway place wanted to pretend they were back in the States, it was all right with him. He'd taken a look at the school and the kids, and had figured out what was going down and had calmly eased himself into the one crowd where there was some action. So what if none of them really belonged anywhere, had any place to call home? It didn't matter if they had assumed an arrogant strut that most Romans thought ridiculous. Joe figured it was their business and he couldn't care less who the hell they thought they were. He was in Rome, and for right now he was sticking with them because they had the action.

The last day, the whole crowd of them were coming down from the top of the Gianicolo hill, some on skateboards, the rest halfway out of the back windows of the big black limo that brought one of them a, nerveless little dark-haired girl named Marcie, to school. The limo was trailing the skateboarders as they took the slow curves down this most lovely of Rome's hills. 'Move your fat ass!' one of the kids in the car yelled as one of the skateboarders narrowly missed a portly woman in a dark dress scurrying to cross the road to safety. Julien, a pale-faced boy with blond curls, tripped off his board, fell awkwardly, and managed to scoop it up and wave for the car to pick him up before it passed by. 'I told you,' someone said when they saw him fall. Julien crawled in, brushing off his well-tailored English jacket, and gave the others a half-apologetic look.

Only one of the skateboarders wore a crash helmet. The others, some trying to do wheelies and 360s, were struggling to take risks. But the road was wide and its slope even, and as they took curve after curve, picking up speed, pedestrians and approaching cars quickly got out of everyone's way.

Joe stood upright on his board, reading the *International Herald Tribune*. The limo came closer to him and somebody leaned out and yelled, 'Get the fuck in here!'

Joe ignored them, and deftly steered his board between two other skateboarders, concentrating on his newspaper.

Another kid fell and the limo slowed, its door opened, and he crawled in.

'Get in,' Marcie called out to Joe, 'come on. Stop reading that stupid thing and get in.'

Joe lowered the paper, saw they had almost come to the bottom of the hill, and hopped off his board. He tossed it into the open door, got in and made himself comfortable on one of the jump seats. Then he opened the newspaper again and began to read, aloud, about the newspaper strike in New York.

'Oh, shut up!' a kid called Scott said to him. 'Who cares about that?'

'Hey, Frances,' Julien said, 'you've been rolling that joint for ages. Is it ready yet?'

'Hold on,' Frances said, concentrating on the loose paper in his hand.

'The Yankees took two more,' Joe said to no one in particular.

Julien was watching Frances, but he was also watching Ariana, a lovely Italian girl with large almond eyes and dark skin. Julien couldn't help himself, he always watched Ariana.

The joint Frances was rolling wasn't marihuana. It was hashish, from Marrakesh, or possibly Morocco. North Africa was nearby, and hashish was readily available, a dark, oily hashish, perfumed and potent. It was like the summer air around them, that curious look and feel which sometimes turned Rome suddenly into more of an African city than European. The limousine with the kids in it was driving past monuments that spoke more of the large dark continent than of Western civilization: elephants, primitive heads, pyramids, palm trees.

Julien moved closer to Ariana, who gave him a look. Valentina saw this and said, 'Hey Julien, when was the last time you pinched Ariana's ass?'

Julien forced a grin, to show he thought this was a terrific joke, and reached for Ariana. 'Right now.'

She made a face and moved out of his way. 'Italian men make me sick,' Valentina said.

'*A bona*!' Frances imitated them, the way they cruised around waiting for some good-looking girl to go by so they could straighten their shoulders and go after her with a 'Hey, sweetheart! Hey, nice ass! Hey, where'ya going?'

'And the way they follow you around in their crappy little Fiats,' Valentina said with exaggerated annoyance which ended with her rolling her eyes upwards.

'I have that problem,' Michelle said.

'You know what you should do?' Marcie said. 'Kick their car.'

'Are you crazy?' Michelle exclaimed. 'I tried that once, the guy wanted to kill me!'

'Too bad he didn't,' Scott said without looking at Michelle.

'Oh, shut up,' she said.

'Hey, hey,' Ted said, 'those guys only love their cars. Their cars and their mammas.'

Joe sat by the window, half listening, staring out. What did these jerks know? he thought to himself. What bullshit!

'They live with their mommies until they're thirty-five,' Michelle was saying.

'Yeah,' Valentina said, 'and they think all other women are whores.'

A few of the crowd broke up at this, laughing and shoving each other with delight. Joe turned to look at them as Frances handed the unrolled joint to him. 'Here,' he said to Joe. 'You roll it.'

Joe started rolling, and abruptly sat forward. 'Driver,' he said, 'would you stop the car, please? Would you please stop the car? Stop the car.'

The big car slowed and pulled over to the kerb. The others looked at Joe with surprise. 'Where you going?' Michelle demanded as Joe started to open the door.

The car stopped and he got out without answering. 'What's with you?' Scott said.

'He's taking off!' someone said and someone else added, 'Hey, we always split!'

Joe turned and looked at them as Marcie gave him a dirty look. 'I think you're being real shitty,' she declared.

'Yeah, what a selfish-rat bastard,' Frances said.

'Here,' Joe said and tossed over the joint, 'you take it. I don't want it.' He closed the car door and started off down the street.

The car moved away in the opposite direction and suddenly stopped. The door opened, and Ariana got out.

Julien watched her as she closed the door, and before the driver could move off again, he quickly opened the other door and scrambled out. 'Hey, Julien!' Scott said. 'You going?'

'So long,' Melissa said.

'Good luck, Julien,' another voice said mockingly. 'Go get her.'

And as the sad-faced boy closed the car door he heard several of his friends laughing.

Ariana caught up to Joe at the corner. When he saw that she had followed him he stopped. 'I'm going with you,' she said.

He looked at her. 'Where?'

'With you,' she repeated, watching his face carefully, uncertain why she found him so fascinating.

Beyond them, Julien kept close to the buildings. He couldn't hear what they were saying and was afraid they might see him.

'I got some things to do,' Joe said.

'If you want,' Ariana said, 'I'll go away.'

'I got nothing against you,' Joe said. 'I mean, I don't even know you.'

'My name is Ariana. I'm Italian.'

'My name's Joe,' he answered. She fell in next to him, and they went off down the street. 'I'm American.' They were on an avenue lined with palm trees and creepers climbing the stone walls. Flowers were in bloom, the air smelled sweet and fresh and the afternoon sun was tropical. Joe looked around and then glanced at Ariana. 'It's like California,' he said, and when she looked at him he nodded his head in the direction of one of the trees they were passing. 'Palm trees.'

'I've never been there,' she said.

'Neither have I,' he admitted, and immediately regretted his admission. They walked further, and he watched her out of the corner of his eye. When he noticed she was doing the same thing, he quickly looked away. 'I've got a girl friend,' he said. 'In New York.'

'That's nice,' Ariana said politely.

Joe nodded, and then said, 'She's a pain in the neck,' adding another admission. 'She's not really my girl friend.'

'Then why are you telling me about her?' Ariana asked.

'I don't know,' Joe said after a moment.

Julien watched them as they went down the street. He saw them get to a movie theatre and slow. Oh, shit, he thought to himself, they're going to go in.

Joe took some money out and shoved it to the ticket-seller. '*Due*,' he said, in Italian.

The ticket-seller gave him the tickets and he turned to Ariana, who was staring at him with a puzzled expression on her face.

'Why do we have to lock ourselves up in a movie theatre?' she said.

'I got to take a wicked piss,' he said and hurried inside.

Ariana ran after him and saw him take a corner and start down the stairs. When she came to the bottom of the stairs, he was gone. She stopped in front of the door with the sign UOMINI – MEN on it, shrugged, and went in.

An old man in baggy pants and a sagging jacket stood at one of the urinals. Joe wasn't in sight, and the doors to all of the stalls were closed.

'Joe!' she called out, and the man turned and saw her. 'Joe, where are you?' She moved from one stall to the next. 'Are you in there? Joe! Where are you? Let me in. Let me in or I'm going to start screaming!'

One of the stall doors suddenly opened and a hand came out and grabbed her and pulled her into the compartment. The old man stared and muttered, '*Oh, Madonna*!' and as he turned and bent to get a better look at the two pairs of feet in the compartment, he started to piss on his own pants. He realized what he was doing and broke into a string of hoarse curses, fumbling to get himself rearranged. He washed his hands, wiped them with paper towel and then wiped his pants, all the time turning to glance over at the closed door of the stall.

'How do we get out of here?' he heard Joe's voice, understanding nothing. 'Damn skateboard!'

The old man got to the door and turned for one last look at the two pairs of feet, heaved a bitter sigh, and walked out.

All became quiet, except for the sounds of breathing behind the stall door. There was a sudden sharp intake of breath – it could have been Joe or Ariana – and then one of them sighed, a child's soft moan of relief, and then once more it was silent.

Some moments passed before the cubicle opened and the two of them came out, Joe carrying the skateboard. They were unsteady on their feet, weak in the knees, and Joe had to help her to the door.

They went upstairs into the theatre itself, and slowed and stared at the pictures flickering up on the screen. They stopped at the back of the house and leaned against the wall. 'How do you feel?' Joe asked. His voice was low, and he felt languid.

'I've never felt so wonderful in my whole life,' Ariana answered, the same slow and loopy tone in her voice. She turned to look at him, her eyes glistening.

'That's the kind of answer a man likes to hear,' Joe said.

Ariana gave a small laugh and put a hand on his chest to steady herself. 'You talk like my father.'

'My father's dead,' Joe said, his eyes on the screen. The music rose to match the turbulent scene of water pouring over a gigantic waterfall. 'You want to sit down?' he asked Ariana.

She suddenly felt terribly weak and reached out for support. 'Wait,' she said, sounding almost drunk. 'I can't—'

'What's wrong?' Joe said and turned to her.

'I don't think I can stand,' she said with sweet helplessness and groped for his hand. 'I'm afraid I'm going to fall down.'

Joe steadied her and said, 'We can sit down right here.' They slid to the carpeted floor at the back wall, Joe with his back to it. He bent his legs and opened them to let Ariana sit comfortably between them and be able to lean comfortably against him. They could both see the screen from where they were, and stared as Marilyn Monroe, fiery in a scarlet dress, came out of a motel room door to join a group of people around a swimming pool. She carried a record in her hand and as she approached two men standing by a record player stopped and stared at her in awe. '*Vorrebe mettere questo*?' she said holding out the record – 'Would you put this one on?'

'When did she ever learn to speak Italian?' Joe said.

On the screen, Marilyn Monroe turned as the music for the song, 'Kiss', began. Her head lifted, and her eyes closed. She didn't notice that Joseph Cotten was watching her through the blinds of the motel room window.

Ariana had leaned back to make herself even more comfortable. Her eyes were closed, she hadn't heard Joe's remark and wouldn't have understood it if she had. She was thinking of other things, and she wanted to talk about it, wanted to tell Joe. 'I've got to tell you something,' she said, and realized it felt dreamlike to talk.

Joe looked at her. 'I already know,' he said.

'No,' she said and gave her head a slow shake, 'you don't. You don't know anything.' She felt very knowledgeable and experienced, and wise with a small special secret. When she felt Joe's hand on her hair, and then his other one come around to hold her, she let herself relax even more.

'It's your first time,' he said.

She wasn't annoyed that he'd guessed. His touch was so soft and his voice sounded so kind, and understanding, she didn't care that he knew. All she wanted was to tell him about it because he understood. 'I feel like everything is right where it should be,' she said, and the words brought the feeling more deeply into her. She could almost see what she felt. 'Oh,' she exclaimed softly, almost sadly, 'if only you could be a part of me. You'd understand.'

'I want to understand,' Joe said, and his caresses intensified. He leaned closer and his mouth was by her ear. 'I want to be inside you.'

'How?' Ariana asked.

'Help me get my jeans off,' he said.

Ariana turned and moved down him a bit and began to undo his belt.

On the screen the song was continuing and Marilyn Monroe turned to two men watching her and in dubbed Italian said, 'It's the only song in the world . . .'

Ariana got the belt open and then undid the top buttons of

Joe's pants and started pulling them down. They slid over his buttocks, and then stuck. She pulled harder, but they wouldn't budge. He wriggled in place and suddenly the pants came free and Ariana pulled them all the way down to his ankles. 'Christ,' he said with momentary embarrassment, 'you didn't have to pull them all the way off!' Ariana stifled a giggle and stared at him, at the dim shape of his legs in the shadows. 'Now yours,' he heard himself say.

'This is the moment,' Monroe was singing on screen, *'oh, kiss . . .'*

Without hesitation, Ariana undid her jeans and pulled them off, all the way. Joe's face registered a moment of shock, and then he couldn't help himself and stared openly at her pale young body. 'You look better than Marilyn Monroe,' he whispered.

A sudden noise a few rows in front of them made them both turn. Someone was noisily climbing out of a row of seats and banging their way up the aisle. Joe nodded towards an opening between the last two rows of seats at the back of the theatre. 'Let's hide there,' he said urgently.

The two of them scrabbled along into the small enclosure, Joe's pants dragging after him, Ariana carrying hers. He slowed and reached back and yanked his skateboard in behind them, and settled close to her, breathing heavily. 'Now what?' she asked uncertainly.

Without hesitation or guile, Ariana took the tooth-brace out of her mouth and then turned her head to his, and with eyes wide open moved closer to him, watching his face and mouth as it approached hers. Joe's lips parted, and then closed, and his lips touched hers and he pressed against her rather than kissed. It was things he'd heard about and she had seen others do; it was moments from movies and giggled exchanges between friends. Then Joe opened his mouth and Ariana opened hers and they pressed harder together and suddenly Joe gasped and pulled away, but immediately returned to kiss her, properly now, intently, seriously passionate.

On the screen, Monroe sang with the record she had put on the record player: '*Kiss me and hold me tight . . .*' She raised her golden head to the cool night air wafting over from the nearby Niagara Falls, and the music was intoxicating.

At the back of the theatre, Joe and Ariana kissed, two children, solemn in their union, determined to make the kiss be correct.

On the screen, Joseph Cotten burst out of the motel room, crossed the lawn to the record player, pushed aside the playing arm, grabbed the record, and smashed it into pieces before the startled eyes of the onlookers. Marilyn Monroe simply watched his desperate act of destruction.

Ariana moved away from Joe, her eyes still wide, and touched her lips which felt sensitive. 'Now,' she said, seeing his eyes on her, 'be inside me.'

'Here?' Joe said, astonished.

'Yes,' she said, and her voice dropped. She felt a bit desperate, because she wanted him to be inside her, because the moment was right, and his kisses, wet and inexperienced, had aroused her. 'Do you know how?' she asked. 'I've never done it.'

'You're excused,' Joe said with an apologetic smile. 'I'm a virgin, too.' He reached for her and caught her by the neck and slowly drew her to him. They began kissing again. His hands touched her shoulders and her arms, and then moved down across her small young breasts. She shivered, and began to touch him . . .

A noise high above them made them both stop, separate, and look up.

The ceiling of the movie theatre was slowly splitting, moving apart, opening to the night sky. The movie had ended – they hadn't noticed when – and now the ceiling was parting with a steady scrape. As more and more of the sky appeared above them, Joe watched, fascinated. And then, above one of the revealed buildings, the moon appeared. Joe stared, and a strange feeling came over him. 'I've got to go,' he said quietly.

'I've got to go.' He reached out blindly, found his jeans, and began to pull them on, unaware that Ariana was staring at him, understanding nothing.

When they came out of the theatre, she stopped and put her brace back in her mouth. Joe watched her and made a face. She saw his crooked incisor, growing at an angle that gave it a beautiful cruel look, and reached out to touch it. 'Why haven't you had it taken out?' she asked.

'I was born with it,' Joe said and moved back just out of her reach, 'and I want to die with it.'

They made their way out of the theatre and found that it was truly evening now. The street lights were lit and passing cars flashed their headlights at intersections. Around them, people were hurrying home from offices and shops. Joe nodded to Ariana, and she was at a loss as to what to say to him. Both were suddenly in a hurry, both were suddenly very shy.

Joe turned and hurried off. Ariana watched him go off down the street, the skateboard balanced under his arm, and then turned and started in the other direction. She saw Julien sitting on the kerb, waiting. His expression was like it always was when he'd waited somewhere for her, a sad little puppy, too tongue-tied to say a thing. She went over to him. He saw her, rose, and fell in by her side. They walked several steps before she said in Italian, 'You want to walk me home?' She didn't turn to him as she said it, and knew Julien wouldn't answer. He would just nod, as he now did, and walk silently with her all the way home.

FOUR

It wasn't so much that the sight of the moon had reminded Joe of something. It had beckoned to him, had drawn him out of the movie house, and led him through crowded Roman streets. There were moments when he would break into a reckless run and for a moment didn't know where he was: was he back in New York? Why did he suddenly think he had come out of one of the side streets into Fifth Avenue? He recognized landmarks, both Roman and from New York, and even when he slowed down and caught his breath and then resumed his way, this strange intermingling of places continued. It didn't frighten him. Skateboard comfortably under his arm, he headed in the same direction. When he heard music, he realized he was not lost. Cathedrals and basilicas and Lincoln Center's mass of buildings and the Colosseum and Rockefeller Center . . . it was all eerily mixed up in his head. When he came to the front of the opera house, Rome's Opera House, it might as well have been the Metropolitan in New York. Above him, the moon still shone, and Joe knew where he was. Without hesitation, he pushed open the doors and went inside. The music grew louder with a warm rush, and then he heard a voice. Caterina's.

His first sight of her was through the glass panel of one of the doors leading into the opera house's orchestra, not where the musicians sat and were playing, but the main floor space for the audience, the parquet. Caterina seemed to be floating in mid-air. Stars glowed around her, and in one corner, brighter than everything else but Caterina, hung a moon. It was not a real moon but it was magical, yellow, full and comforting.

The opera was still in its first act – it was *Il Trovatore*, 'The Troubador' – and Caterina was singing the role of Leonora. '*Listen!*' she sang in this aria where she told how she has fallen in love with a mysterious troubador who has appeared to sing to her, '. . . *The moon showed its full and silvery face, when in the air, so still till then, the sweet and sad sounds of a lute were heard, and sad verses were sung by a troubador.*' Joe slowly pushed through into the hall, and leaned against the wooden side of the stairwell. He could feel the hundreds of pairs of eyes riveted to Caterina as she continued to sing, describing the way Leonora felt when she heard the troubador's melancholy voice and spoke her name. '*I sped to the balcony,*' she went on, '*and it was he, there he was!*'

Behind Joe, an elderly man, wizened but still aristocratic-looking, turned to his wife and said in Italian, 'Did you remember to turn out the lights before we went out?'

Joe whirled and hissed, 'Shhh!' and then turned back muttering to himself, 'Fucking asshole . . .'

On stage, Caterina began slowly to float down as she was completing the aria. As her feet touched the stage the last notes sounded and the hall exploded into applause. She barely acknowledged it, a slight tilt of the head, no more than that, accompanied by a pause in the music, and then she slowly moved off stage as a scrim rose to reveal a magnificent waterfall with water cascading down steps from high at the back of the stage. It was an extraordinary sight, and for a moment there was a hush in the audience, as if to allow them time to absorb the impact of the setting before them. Then the music resumed, and the count, the Count di Luna, appeared, and began to sing about the stillness of the night and his own turbulent feelings. He sang of his love for Leonora, and his burning jealousy for this unknown troubador who had captured her heart.

Joe slowly backed down the steps, and made his way around the back of the hall to the door leading backstage. He came up behind five men handling ropes with which they were slowly lowering a sky-blue backdrop. He slowed and had to close his eyes as sweat appeared on his forehead. He wiped it off, took a deep breath, and continued. He came to one side of the stage, across from where Caterina had made her exit. He could see the waterfall closer now, but it wasn't a real one at all. Five men slowly turned enormous rollers on to which strips of silvery paper had been fastened. As the rollers turned, the paper turned with it, flopping irregularly over to produce the very real effect of falling water.

The sound of a harp made Joe turn and he saw a harpist playing as, nearby, a man in costume began to sing. This was the Troubador, Il Trovatore of the opera's title, singing about his hope for the love of Leonora. On stage, the Count was hearing these words and his rage was growing. Joe moved carefully past where the Troubador sang and saw Caterina preparing to return on to the stage. He saw her step uncertainly out on to the stage, her uncertainty Leonora's, who has heard the voice of her Troubador. Joe moved back, and leaned his head against a flat. The sweat was back and he had to close his eyes again. Leonora was singing again, interrupted by the deep voice of the Count. Then Leonora answered, and the uncertainty was in her voice as she realized she had mistaken the cloaked figure of the Count for her Troubador. Joe heard a man's voice nearby say, under his breath but distinctly: '*Avvampo di furor* . . .' It was the prompter, score before him, mouthing each line, conducting the music with his free hand as his eyes stayed glued to the singers on the stage. '*Avvampo di furor!*' the Count was singing on stage almost precisely in unison with the prompter.

'*Io t'amo! Io t'amo!*' the prompter pronounced.

'*I love you! I love you!*' Leonora was swearing to her as yet unidentified Troubador on stage as he tried to recover from his shock of seeing her tell the Count (his hated enemy) that she loved him.

The tempo quickened, the prompter conducted more quickly, and the words spilled out of all three singers as the danger grew and the melodrama heightened.

Joe turned and made his way down to Caterina's dressing room. He heard the music clearly, the Count learning that the Troubador was Manrico, Manrico welcoming the Count's challenge, Leonora begging the both of them to be reasonable. He closed the door of the dressing room and looked around. There were flowers everywhere, some in vases, others wrapped in cellophane, others in thin green paper, lying arranged on the divan like ears of corn. There was a small loudspeaker above her dressing table and he could hear the music continue. At the other end of the small room was a rack with Caterina's costumes hanging up. Her dressing table was a jumble of open make-up jars and tins. He put his skateboard on top of everything and sat down. Someone had left some champagne in a glass and he picked it up and took a drink. It had gone flat and sour and he spat it out.

Exhaustion suddenly overtook him and he could feel his eyes stinging. He wanted to hide. He got up and moved around the room. Behind a screen he found a big leather armchair. He crawled on to it, pulled a piece of cloth over his head, and closed his eyes. The music was still there, and he heard it growing to a climax. There was a sudden explosion of applause, long and sustained, like warm thunder. Then he fell asleep.

The sound of voices awoke him. He opened his eyes and peered through a crack in the screen in front of the chair. The door to the dressing room was open and a press of people was trying to get inside. Caterina was in their centre, glowing, turning this way and that to accept their congratulations. The admirers were congratulating her as well as calling out to each other, as if this place was the first moment they had realized they were all at the performance together. 'Champagne!' someone yelled and corks popped as someone else was shouting '*Brava! Brava! Stupendo!*'

'*Fuori! Fuori!* – Out! Out!' a tall, handsome woman began to shout and started trying to shoo everyone out of the small room. Nobody moved.

'Caterina!' one man cried, almost tragically, looking ready to throw himself at Caterina's feet. He never managed to get even close to her because someone else appeared and insisted they had to kiss her, had to thank her with their adoration, simply *had* to. They drew close and the tall woman who was trying to get everybody out of the room stepped in between the man and Caterina and shook her head, muttering something about who did he think he was, endangering Caterina with a cold by kissing her! 'Caterina has to change!' she turned to shout at everyone. 'Out! Out!'

Miraculously, with the champagne being toasted and the milling bodies, people actually began to leave. '*Wonderful!*' a tall American cried to her as he was forced to back out of the room. He raised his glass to Caterina and was out the door, the last seen of him the glass in the doorway waggling from side to side.

When the door finally closed, the only ones left in the room were Caterina, her maid, and Marina, who had somehow managed to slip in as the others were being chased out. Caterina was sweating and felt very hot and began to fan herself, crying, '*Acqua, acqua!*' She waved at her maid to get her something to drink and repeated it: '*Acqua, acqua, acqua . . . !*'

'Caterina,' Marina said, visibly moved. 'Your voice . . .' Caterina accepted her embrace and accepted a glass of champagne from her maid. 'You have never sung so well,' Marina went on. 'Your voice is beautiful!'

'I know,' Caterina agreed and took a drink. She sat down before her dressing table, and then pushed back so she could look up at Marina. 'I held that D flat for nine measures.' It wasn't a boast, it was a fact, and she knew she'd given a splendid performance and had the right to tell people she damn well knew she'd been good. 'My breath seems endless.'

'I don't understand about B flat,' Marina admitted.

'D!' Caterina said.

'D. B,' Marina said, and shrugged. 'All I know is that since Douglas died you are singing much better.' She stared at Caterina, and added, 'You've grown.'

Their eyes met, and Caterina knew Marina understood. 'Stronger, Marina,' she said. 'Stronger.' Memories suddenly crowded in on her – the first time Marina had come to meet her, the growth of their friendship, how Douglas had admitted his own affections for Marina, the last time they had all been together in a dressing room like this one after Caterina had sung in the same opera . . .

Her hairdresser, Jole, came in, asking in Italian if Caterina would let her take off the wig.

Caterina nodded and turned to her mirror. Her face looked back at her, the make-up smeared, a shadow of her character barely visible. Weariness overtook her and she had to close her eyes. 'I feel so old,' she said quietly.

There was a sudden commotion at the door and the maid hurried over and stopped it from opening further, shouting in Italian that they had to stop instantly what they were doing, it wasn't allowed. She went so far as to excuse herself for being so strict, but no one was to enter. 'Please,' she begged the throng outside the door, 'you may not come in.'

'Can't we come in?' a fan cried, and others picked up the call. 'Please, let us in.' The maid shook her head one more time and closed the door on them. Behind it, she heard a disappointed moan.

Marina stared at Caterina, who sat at her dressing table, her head in one hand. 'Don't be silly. Old? You're stunning. Everyone adores you.'

Jole unpinned the wig and started to take it off when Caterina winced. 'Ai!' she exclaimed, and in Italian said, 'Watch it, Jole. You're hurting me.' She let the wig be lifted off her head, and began to fluff out her own hair. She saw Marina watching her in the mirror and said, 'I was great tonight,' and once again saw her own face reflected before her. There were lines there, around the eyes and even at the corners of her mouth. 'It's all Joe's fault.' One of her hands touched the corner of an eye. 'If only he'd stop growing, I wouldn't be so old.'

'Right,' Marina agreed diplomatically. 'What about tomorrow?'

'Tomorrow?'

'Joe's birthday,' Marina said, and saw Caterina's expression change. 'You forgot!'

'Oh, God!' Caterina cried in despair. 'Oh shit! How could I forget? Oh, Marina, I'm terrible, I don't remember anything.' She stopped suddenly and stared at herself in the mirror, hating herself, overcome by sudden guilt. Yet at the same time she was angry, angry at Joe for having this birthday she hadn't remembered.

'You forgot,' Marina said, not wanting Caterina to go overboard with self-pity.

'I feel sick,' Caterina said bitterly. 'I hate birthdays.' She stood up and turned to implore Marina. 'You know I was nervous tonight. I was scared. It's the first time I've sung here in years. I knew that audience was out to get me, they were listening for every note.' She began to take off her outer costume and, as she spoke, she pulled it off and slipped on a dressing gown. 'I was a little bit shaky at first,' she was admitting. 'The first few notes, they weren't solid.' It was almost a defensive routine for her, going over her performance like a coach meeting with his team to look at action replays. Caterina needed it, she knew it helped her. Douglas wasn't there to do it for her any more, so if he wasn't going to be taking care of her singing, her voice, who the hell could do it for her? Nobody. Oh Jesus, the first notes were wobbly, and that audience was out to get her. 'They didn't notice anything,' she said angrily. 'They loved it. I've never seen anything like it. It was incredible!' She turned, and leaned over to fix her make-up in the mirror. She saw herself, and remembered Joe, that it was his birthday, and that he had missed her triumph. 'Poor Joe,' she said, almost to herself.

Marina heard and went over to put an arm around her shoulder. 'Don't worry,' she said. 'I've already ordered a cake. I will take care of everything.'

'I want a lot of people at Joe's birthday,' she said. 'I want him to feel important, I want him to feel loved.'

Joe had had it by then, and got out of the chair and stepped from behind the screen. The maid saw him and gave a start, dropping a dress she held on a hanger, and cried, 'Ah!'

'I only want a few people at my party,' he said curtly.

Caterina whirled and saw him. 'Joe!'

Marina was clutching herself. 'Joe,' she said, 'you scared the hell out of me!'

Caterina stared, and it took her a few moments to figure out he'd heard everything between her and Marina. She was annoyed, and so her feelings of guilt became mixed with genuine anger. 'Where have you been?' she demanded. 'You promised you'd be here. I needed you!' She was warming to it, but she was going to let him know exactly how she felt. 'God only knows how I got through the performance without you.'

'I heard ten minutes of applause,' Joe said and gave her a knowing look.

She returned it, and then straightened up, deciding he wasn't going to get smart with her, and with a shake of her shoulders said, 'Actually, it was a standing ovation.' She was glad he'd heard that applause, and she was even happier to have him there with her. Her anger melted and she went over and put her arms around him. 'Joe, you're a naughty boy!' She kissed him on one cheek and then the other.

Joe pulled away and began to wipe his face automatically. 'Lay off, Mom, you're getting lipstick all over me.'

Caterina's hand rose to wipe off any smudges and then she saw there were none. 'I didn't,' she said.

'I just want a few people at my party,' he said. 'My friends, Bobby, Ariana . . .'

'Darling,' Caterina said, softening, 'I understand, of course.' She was eager to please him, to get over the shame of having forgotten. 'People who really love you.'

'People who really love me,' Joe said, staring at her levelly, 'don't forget my birthday.'

Caterina returned his gaze, thinking, I know he's mad at me, but why is he being such a little prick about it? He knows how I feel, so why is he rubbing it in? 'How long have you been here?' she said.

Marina sensed the rise in tension and came over to Joe. 'Darling,' she said dramatically, hoping it would make him laugh, 'please forgive me if I don't come to your party but I have a very important rendezvous.'

'Oh, Marina,' Joe said with a sarcastic look on his face, 'you're breaking my heart.'

Caterina wanted to snap at him because Marina was being

very considerate, when the door burst open and the baritone who had sung the Count appeared, hopping unsteadily on one foot as he struggled to pull off one of his boots. '*Ci sono . . .*' he began in Italian: 'There're eighty people already invited and I'm serving four kinds of spaghetti.'

Marina started to laugh helplessly as the baritone continued hopping about, the boot stuck on his foot. 'I'll have to change,' Caterina said to him.

'Bring your son,' the singer said in his deep voice as he hopped out the door, 'he's a good lad.'

'What'd he say?' Joe said.

Caterina translated what the singer had said, adding, 'He wants you to come.'

'I don't want to.'

Caterina came over and confronted him. 'Joe,' she said, 'stop acting like a baby.'

'I told you,' Joe said, his expression sullen, 'I'm not coming. And don't call me a baby. I hate parties, I hate your friends. I can't stand any more spaghetti.' He pulled away from her and walked across the tiny room.

Caterina came over and faced him. She put both hands on his shoulders and firmly pushed him back until he had to sit down on the divan. He half turned because he was going to crush some of the flowers, but his mother wouldn't let him. 'You listen to me,' she said. 'Every time I try to talk to you, you look away.' She made sure he was listening, sitting there, uncomfortably trying to get the flowers out from under him, but listening. She went over, behind the changing screen, and started to change into her evening dress. 'You go into hiding,' she went on.

'You're the one hiding,' Joe said.

Caterina stopped what she was doing, and came part way out from behind the screen to look at him. 'Yes, maybe I am,' she admitted. She looked at him for several moments more, and then returned behind the screen to continue changing. 'If I am,' she said, 'it's because I really don't know how to talk to you. Since we've been in Italy, you seem distant, and strange.'

Joe wasn't listening. The moment she went back behind the screen, he switched off, and let his attention wander. When there was a knock on the door he jumped to his feet, relieved to have some sort of interruption before his mother really got going with some sort of bullshit. 'I'll get it,' he said and opened the door. 'Hello!'

A young man stood there, limply elegant, holding a tiny bunch of flowers. He had one of those weak aristocratic faces, and looked as if he'd inadvertently done something he shouldn't have. 'Hello,' he said hesitantly to Joe, and moved past him into the room. It was almost a glide, and as he passed Joe noticed his tailored white linen slacks, the fawn vest, and the silk shirt. He had a couple of silk scarves tossed around his neck, and a raincoat hung on his shoulders. 'Oh, Marina!' he exclaimed almost with relief when he saw her.

'Edward!' Marina said.

Edward looked around, looking more distressed than ever. 'Where is Caterina?' There was apprehension in his voice, though he spoke with the fine upper-class drawl of the well-educated Englishman.

'Edward,' Caterina called out from behind the screen and rose on tiptoe to peer over it. Edward saw it and moved closer, his head lifting as he came closer. He was trembling, like a thin reed, as he came just close enough for the lips to touch, and then, still trembling, he stepped back to gaze at her. 'I'll be with you in a minute,' she said quietly.

'Okay,' he said, and let himself look around. The heat seemed to settle around him because perspiration appeared suddenly on his brow. He took out a yellow silk handkerchief and dabbed his forehead. 'Jesus,' he said with delicate complaint, 'it is hot in here.'

'I think you need a drink,' Marina suggested.

'Take off your coat,' Joe suggested.

Edward glanced at him, unsure who this curious kid might be, and then Marina appeared with a large frosted glass which she handed him.

'Your drink.'

He took a sip, and then two more in quick succession, his eyes roaming the room, settling finally on the make-up mirror with its telegrams. 'My God, look at the telegrams . . .'

'Read them to me,' Caterina said from behind the screen.

Edward approached the mirror, continuing to take small sips, and leaned over to stare at several of the messages. His lips moved soundlessly as he skimmed a few, and then he stopped.

'Who's Leo?'

'Leo could be anybody,' Caterina answered. She took a quick look at him because she had sensed his discomfort. 'How was I, Edward?'

A pained expression appeared on his face and he carefully put the glass down on her make-up table before turning to address the unseen person behind the screen. 'The plane was two fucking hours late,' he said, surrendering completely. 'I'm terribly sorry, I missed the performance.'

Marina retrieved his glass and held it up for him to see. 'Another drink?'

'I only just managed to pull myself together,' he said, and nodded to Marina that yes, he most definitely wanted another drink.

Caterina appeared suddenly from behind the screen, radiant, glowing, stunning in a flowing gown. Her maid stared and clapped her hands with delight. '*Come bella!*' she exclaimed in Italian – 'How beautiful! How beautiful'

But Caterina was staring at Edward as he stood before her in all his studied elegance. 'You did a wonderful job of pulling yourself together,' she said with a nod.

Edward let himself wilt, and drew his shoulders down, forlorn and apologetic. 'Did you take the D flat tonight?'

Caterina's eyes narrowed and she smiled victoriously. 'You blew it, Edward.'

Destroyed, he was on the verge of falling to his knees before her. 'Caterina,' he wailed, 'you know I adore you.'

'People who adore me,' Caterina said, 'don't miss my opening nights,' and threw a sharp look at her son. 'Right, Joe?'

Edward, humiliated, collapsed grandly into a chair. He

covered his eyes with one hand, and stretched out his long legs. 'I'm finished,' he uttered very privately, very dramatically.

Joe looked from his mother at the sprawling figure of Edward, and started for the door.

'Where are you going?' Marina said.

'Actually,' he said, and couldn't help imitating Edward's refined accent, 'I have to take a fart.'

Caterina snickered, but Marina took it seriously and gestured for Joe to slow down. 'Wait a second,' she said, because she thought he might be trying to get out of there. She had something very important to tell him and she wanted him to appreciate it. 'Do you know what it means in Italy when you are fifteen?'

This stopped Joe cold, and he stared at her a moment before answering. 'What?'

Marina puffed herself up just a tiny bit, and with a solemn look in her eye declared, 'It means you are no longer fourteen.'

'Big deal,' Joe said, 'it means the same thing in America.' He went over and opened the door and found himself staring at a small, stockily built woman in an enormous dress and flowered hat.

'Caterina!' the woman exclaimed and charged in, followed by a *portiere* carrying a gigantic basket of mixed fruits and flowers. She waved for the flowers to be brought along as she charged towards Caterina, crying, 'You were marvellous! Wonderful!'

'Ludovica,' Caterina said and backed off as Ludovica made to throw her arms around her. 'Thank you, thank you.'

Ludovica abruptly whirled and gestured to the basket of fruits and flowers. 'For you! Special for you!'

Caterina helped herself to a grape. 'How delicious, Ludovica,' she said.

'How expensive, my dear,' Ludovica unhesitatingly qualified, and immediately headed for Caterina, intending to grab her all over again. 'Caterina, shall we have supper tomorrow, you and I?'

Caterina deftly evaded her, doing a small pirouette. 'I can't.'

'Then the day after tomorrow,' Ludovica said, pursuing patiently.

Caterina crossed the small room and turned back to the approaching woman. 'I can't,' she said sweetly. 'I'm doing something.'

Ludovica came closer, but stopped because she didn't want Caterina evading her eternally. 'Let's make it Thursday,' she said reasonably.

'Thursday,' Caterina said thoughtfully, and seemed to remember something. 'I can't Thursday, I'm busy.'

'You cannot?' Ludovica said, not at all disappointed. 'Then tonight. Let's make it tonight.'

'Tonight I'm having supper with my son,' Caterina said and indicated Joe, who was off to one side, watching the brief exchange between his mother and this weird-looking woman.

'You never give up, do you Ludovica?' Edward's voice interrupted. Ludovica turned and saw him as if for the first time.

'Eduardo!' she said.

He rose languidly and came over to link arms with her. 'Caterina has made it quite clear she cannot have supper with either of us.' He moved her away from Caterina, towards the door. 'So, let's have supper together.'

'Okay,' Ludovica said with a sigh of resignation, and then managed to brighten. 'With pleasure.' She moved to the door with renewed energy and turned to bid Caterina goodbye. 'Ciao, Caterina,' she called.

Caterina gave her a wave and went over to Edward. She leaned close to him and said, 'You're wonderful in emergencies.' She gave him a kiss and he hurried out after Ludovica, closing the door behind him.

'Now you know what I have to put up with, Joe,' she said, turning back to him. 'You're the only person who can protect me in these situations.'

'You're doing all right, Mom.'

'Joe, darling, you must learn to humour me, to humour my vanity.' She made a wan gesture; her shoulders fell perceptibly, and she let him see her weakness. 'I know I have faults,' she admitted. 'God knows. You know them, you know my weaknesses.' He listened, but his face still tried to show nothing. 'If you'd laugh at me now and then,' she went on, 'I'd be thrilled.' She meant it sincerely, with all her heart, and Joe regarded her with a small smile. Caterina broke into a broad smile, and said, 'I'd be in heaven.' She added a laugh, and Joe's face parted into a grin. She came over to him and faced him, like a fighter who has some tough news to share. 'I have been through a night that would torture man – ' Joe grinned more broadly, ' – woman – ' he laughed, ' – dog . . .' She could have kept her list going, but she didn't have to. Joe was laughing. With her.

FIVE

Marina did more than arrange for Joe's birthday cake. She rented the terraces of one of Rome's loveliest restaurants, and when Joe arrived, small tables had been set up on one of them, while the other was decorated and left open for dancing. Caterina, nervously enthusiastic that everything go right, was all over the place, fussing. Joe was annoyed when she began advising everybody which table they should sit at, and then she began to nag the waiters about being slow to bring the food. When there was a sound of guitar music, Caterina jumped to her feet and rushed to the terrace's railing and looked down at the street below. Three girls, two carrying guitars, were playing and singing. 'Girls! Girls!' Caterina called out to them. 'Come up here.' She turned to Joe, looking triumphant, as if the most marvellous coincidence had just occurred. 'They're down there, these girls, like angels . . .' She turned back and waved once more. 'Up here. You'll have a wonderful time. It's my son's birthday.'

Moments later the three girls, all of them Americans – Joe had seen them singing and playing in front of some of the deluxe hotels – came out from inside the restaurant and came up the steps to the lower of the two terraces.

'Hey, great,' a boy named Scott said when he saw the girls with their guitars, 'we're going to have some music.'

Caterina, looking more flushed than ever, came back to the table where Joe was sitting. She carried a champagne glass in her hand and used it to wave in the direction of the girls. 'They've come to play for you,' she said, and then looked around, as if the beauty of her surroundings had suddenly affected her and she had to stop and catch her breath. 'Joe, Joe . . . such beautiful girls.' She pretended not to notice his surly expression and turned to look over her shoulder as she heard the sounds of guitar music. 'They've come to play for you,' she repeated.

'Ma,' Joe said, 'don't shit me. You know you arranged it.'

Caterina turned back and fixed him with a level stare. 'I want to tell you something,' she said and peered at him and leaned closer to make her words more intimate. 'When I was fifteen, I was miserable, really miserable.' She was making herself remember the way she'd been at that age, and for a moment it worked and she forgot the frowning boy in front of her. 'I used to lock myself in the bathroom and think about killing myself.'

'Really?' Joe said, a bit impressed.

Caterina straightened and the memory, true or manufactured, disappeared and she took a sip of her champagne as she said, 'When you're fifteen, it's not so bad to be miserable.'

'Mom,' Joe began, wanting to say something to her, but didn't because she rose and began to sway rhythmically to the music the trio was playing.

'Makes me want to cry,' she said wistfully. She stopped and turned and saw that the three girls were still on the lower terrace. 'Girls,' she called, 'you're in the wrong place. Come up here. We want to dance.' She continued to move to the approaching sounds, the glass in her hand. 'In the sixties,' she began, her expression lost in memory, 'we believed in . . . things.' She whirled, and came closer to Joe and reached out to him. 'Come on.' She pulled him to his feet, though he resisted.

'I don't like dancing,' he said through clenched teeth, aware that all of his friends were watching, amused.

Caterina let go of him and he slumped back in his chair while she continued her languid solo. 'When I was fifteen,' she was saying, 'I hated sunshine. I adored darkness. And I stopped believing in God.' Joe saw his friends listening to her. He wasn't sure what they thought, because some had smiles on their faces. Maybe they were just being polite. He didn't care, he just wished she'd shut the hell up. 'My parents thought they understood me, but they didn't.' Caterina was looking down at Ariana, who returned her look with a nod. 'I pitied them,'

Caterina said, and her expression grew sad. Just as suddenly, she brightened and was back in front of Joe, reaching out to him. 'Come on, Joe. Dance. Let's get a little action.' She saw she couldn't budge him, and moved back a few steps to survey the tables of Joe's friends. Ariana walked by and Caterina watched her go and then said, 'You're such stick-in-the-muds. Come on,' she encouraged all of them. 'Dance!' She turned away from them and headed for the three musicians. 'Oh, you're too young to have any fun.' She took a sip from her glass and realized it was empty. 'I'm thirsty.' She didn't see Joe get up and follow Ariana.

Ariana was on the lower terrace. Joe saw her and said, 'God, I hate her.' His eyes flashed as he looked back to where she had been dancing. He leaned closer to Ariana. 'I could kill her.'

Ariana wasn't at all shocked. 'Come on,' she said to him. 'She's fantastic. She's such fun.'

On the other terrace, Caterina decided she really wanted to dance. 'Hi,' she said to Julien, 'what's your name?'

'Julien,' he answered, and blushed.

'Julien,' Caterina said and held out her hand, 'would you like to dance with me, Julien?'

A couple of the kids smirked as Julien forced himself to meet Caterina's gaze. 'Actually, I don't know how to dance,' he said, almost stammering. 'I really don't know how.'

Caterina took his hand and the boy had to get up, though he resisted. 'I'm not going to hurt you,' she assured him. 'Come, I'll teach you.'

Joe watched his mother lead Julien out on to the dance floor. She showed him how to hold her hand, and tried to start dancing.

'Look at Julien,' Ariana said. 'He's dancing! Look at him, look at him.'

Joe turned. Julien was trying to lead Caterina in a disco move he must have seen someone else do. Caterina was trying to hold on to his hand and dance with him. Julien was being thrown off balance, and had to move clumsily from one foot to the other. 'The Incredible Hulk,' Joe said. 'God, is she pathetic!'

'She's just happy,' Ariana said. 'You're ashamed of her, that's all.'

'Ashamed!' Joe flared angrily. 'What do you mean, ashamed?' He turned and stared back at his mother as she made Julien twirl awkwardly. He got to his feet and grabbed Ariana's hand. 'Come,' he said, 'let's go. Let's get out of here.' He turned and went off towards the stairs leading off the terrace to the street, Ariana behind him.

A moment later a trolley with a cake on it was wheeled out by a waiter. There were fifteen candles on it, burning, and some of the kids started to sing 'Happy Birthday'. Caterina hurried back to the table, Julien dragging along behind her. 'Where's Joe?' she asked, and looked around. 'Joe!' she called.

'Where is he?' Marcie said, and half rose out of her chair to crane her neck.

The trolley got to the table and the waiter stood by, waiting patiently. The candles continued to burn.

'I saw him just a minute ago,' Michelle said.

'Joe!' Scott cried. 'Joe!'

Caterina looked around, and then went to look over the railing at the edge of the terrace.

There was a small courtyard below them, off the street which fronted the restaurant itself. She could see Joe and Ariana, in the shadows of a small niche. They were huddled close to one another. Caterina smiled to herself, and turned to go after them.

Down in the courtyard, she approached slowly. They were still so close to each other – she was moved and almost shocked at the intensity of their intimacy; it must have been more than just necking, and the thought actually thrilled her. She had considered surprising them, the way one of their friends might do it, but then she saw their heads move closer together once more and she knew she wouldn't embarrass them. It was Joe's birthday, though, and she did want him to come back and join his friends. She took a few more steps to them, and saw the space between them as Ariana took a step back.

They weren't necking. Ariana had been using her hand instead of a tourniquet to squeeze Joe's upper arm. Joe had a hypodermic needle in his hand and the needle was fixed into his vein. Caterina stopped, paralysed, and as the picture froze itself into her mind for ever, her world collapsed. She stared at the two children who were frozen in the intensity of the fix and knew it was a moment she could never forget. 'I like holding your arm,' she heard Ariana say, and then the girl looked up and saw Caterina watching them. Her expression emptied but she did not jerk away. All she did was quietly say, 'Your mother.' Her eyes returned to Joe for a moment – he was staring intently down at the spike in his arm – and she repeated, 'Your mother.' She let go of his arm, and slowly walked by Caterina as Joe raised his head and saw his mother.

Caterina moved past Ariana, blind to her presence, and as Joe withdrew the needle from his arm Caterina grabbed it and began to smash it against the stone wall. Joe did nothing, said nothing.

When there was nothing left of the hypo, Caterina grabbed him by the hand and dragged him back with her, past Ariana again, back to the restaurant. As they came through the inside dining room and came out on to the lower terrace, they heard the singing, '*Happy birthday to you . . .*'

They climbed the stairs to the upper terrace and Caterina let go of Joe's hand and left him to stand some distance from the table and his friends, who were continuing to sing:

'*Happy birthday to you . . .*'

Caterina seemed oblivious to them. She hurried to where she had been sitting, grabbed her purse, and returned to where Joe stood waiting.

'*Happy birthday dear Joe, Happy birthday to you.*'

She took his hand and they hurried back down towards the main terrace as behind them Joe's friends burst into happy applause. Joe followed with a strange docility. His body seemed to have gone soft, become pliant.

When they came out of the restaurant, Joe walked right past their waiting car. The driver had the door opened and as Joe passed he gave him a curious look and then turned to Caterina who was hurrying to catch up. She threw a desperate look after Joe as he moved off down the street and then looked back at the driver, who stood waiting, a questioning expression on his face. '*Poi tornare a casa,*' she told him – 'You can go back to the house. We're going to walk.'

When they came out on to the embankment along the Tiber, Joe was several yards ahead, walking steadily, pace even, head a bit down. Caterina broke into a small trot several times to catch up, and at one point called out, 'Joe, Joe . . .' He didn't bother to turn. 'Would you please slow down?' He ignored her completely, and abruptly crossed the street, dodging the small cars whizzing by. Caterina, trapped on the pavement, stepped out gingerly, and frightened by the swift-moving traffic made a dash to join him on the other side, once more calling out to him, 'Joe, Joe, Joe!'

They walked this way into the Piazza Farnese, empty of cars and full of young people. There was one group tossing a baseball back and forth, and another congregated by a small ice-cream stand. A couple of the kids saw Joe and hurried over to him. 'Hey, Joe,' one boy called out. Joe turned but didn't slow down.

'Hi, Joe,' a pretty girl called.

'Come and have a drink,' the boy said.

'I can't,' Caterina heard Joe answer and continue walking across the Piazza. 'I gotta go.'

He was nearing the street leading out of the Piazza when a boy on a Vespa motorscooter came by, spotted Joe, and did a neat turn to pass him once more, reaching out so the two could exchange palm-slap greetings.

'Mustafa!' Caterina heard her son say, 'how ya doin'?'

The boy on the scooter continued to circle Joe as he walked along. They exchanged some more words – Caterina heard none of it – and then the boy straightened his machine and headed in his original direction, past Caterina to whom he flashed a broad smile. She saw then his round face, framed in beautiful black curls. There was something exotic in his complexion, which was a dark olive, and his eyes, long-lashed and large, were almost black. When Caterina looked back, Joe was far ahead of her, turning a corner.

She followed him that way all the way to their apartment building. The apartment was in an old Roman building, in old Rome. Its courtyard, full of palm trees and overgrown with tropical vegetation, looked as if it might have been in Bombay. The doors led off the inner courtyard. Joe was still ahead of Caterina, and he walked over to one of the doors and stopped. Caterina went to the other door and then looked at him, standing before the first door. 'Where are you going?' she said, and rang the bell. Joe looked at her and then at the door in front of him, and reached out and rang the bell. 'Jesus God,' Caterina said softly, terribly upset. 'Don't scare me like this. Joe, don't you even remember where we live?'

The two doors opened simultaneously and Caterina found herself facing a ten-year-old girl she'd never seen before. Shocked, she took a step back and in Italian hurriedly said, 'I got the wrong door, sorry!' She backed off farther and indicated the one where Joe stood, their maid, Concetta, holding it open. 'I live here,' Caterina went on explaining to the girl who listened rather indifferently, 'next door.' She turned and disappeared into her own apartment. Joe followed her and the maid shut the door. The little girl shrugged, and went back into her own apartment as a woman's voice called out in Italian, 'Who was that?'

The little girl answered, in Italian, 'It's those Americans next door,' and closed the door.

Caterina's apartment was enormous, with a large central room much like a converted painter's studio, which led out to a small inner garden. The apartment's rooms led off either directly from the large room or the garden. There wasn't much furniture yet and what was there looked as if it'd been rearranged several times, to suit moods of the moment rather than interior designs.

Joe started across the living room towards the door of his own room but Caterina called out, 'Joe!' and made him stop. He turned as Concetta came in. '*Chiude le porte* – Close the doors,' Caterina told her. Joe sat down on the large grey couch and waited. There was a coffee table in front of him, with a large bowl of hard candies. He took one of the sweets, unwrapped it, and put it in his mouth. Then he took another piece and pitched it into an ashtray. It slipped out. He tried again. There was a *bing!* sound and the candy flipped out on to the table. Caterina meanwhile had taken off her shoes and was pacing, trying to fix herself somehow to be able to talk to him. It didn't seem to be working because she slowed abruptly and simply said, 'Why do you do it?'

Joe didn't bother to answer, and noisily cracked the sweet between his teeth.

Caterina, unnerved, looked around. She saw that large drapes had been hung to cover the doors which led out to the small garden. 'They finally put up the curtains,' she said conversationally, and gestured. She went over – she was trying to make talk with him, trying to get some sort of an answer out of him, and nothing was working – and pulled the cord on the drapes and they parted. An upholsterer was on a ladder behind them, hanging half upside down, adjusting something. When the curtains opened he lost his grip and began to fall off the ladder. Caterina gave a small exclamation and took a step back.

'*Buongiorno*,' the man greeted her politely, scrambling to regain his hold on the ladder, and then added, in Italian, 'Am I bothering you?'

'No,' Caterina answered, after she'd managed to collect herself. 'No, go ahead and finish.' She re-closed the curtains and went back and sat down in front of Joe. 'Won't you even talk to me?' she said. Joe remained silent. Caterina forced herself to stay in control, and once more looked around. Her eyes lighted on the material the upholsterer was tacking up. 'I hate that colour,' she observed, and then added, louder, in Italian, for the upholsterer's benefit, 'Excuse me' – his head appeared – 'I hate that colour. I don't like it.'

The workman cocked his head philosophically and leaned away from the material to examine it. 'That's a shame,' he answered in Italian, 'because it's lovely.' He rolled up the drapes on their standard, lifted them off their hooks, and carried them down off the ladder, shaking his head mournfully.

'I'm sorry,' Caterina told him in Italian.

'I'm going to go,' he answered her. 'I'm really going to go.' Without a backward glance, he manoeuvred the drapes out of the door, and was gone.

Joe was still sitting on the couch, pitching sweets into the ashtray. 'When did you start?' she asked him. He looked up at her, and slowly collapsed face down on to the couch, spreading his hands to make a loud *whumping* noise.

The telephone rang – it was the house intercom – and Caterina picked it up and, when she heard Concetta's voice, said, 'We're not home to anyone. Not even Marina.' Caterina turned back to Joe; the interruptions were starting to drive her crazy and she was desperate to talk to him. 'Joe,' she began anew, 'Joey, please tell me what I've done to you? Don't be afraid.' He said nothing. 'You won't hurt me,' she added. Still nothing from him. She took a cigarette from a box on a nearby table and looked for a match or a lighter. 'Could I have a light?' she asked him evenly. He didn't respond. 'Could I have a light?' she repeated. 'Could I have a light?' He moved, finally, as she continued to repeat, 'Could I have a light, could I have a light, *could I have a light*?' He picked up the lighter on a nearby table and held it for her. When she had inhaled on her cigarette, she blew the smoke out, contemplated the tiny ash growing on the end of the cigarette, and said, 'Who gave you that stuff, that fat-assed little hippie friend of yours?'

Joe had put the lighter back and went over to where a television set was sitting on the floor. Without reacting to her remark, he kicked viciously at the screen, shattering it.

Caterina, frightened, jumped to her feet. 'Joe,' she cried, 'what are you doing to me?'

He whirled on her now, ready to say something, when Concetta appeared out in the garden, followed by several large men hefting something enormous. 'Madame,' Concetta said politely in Italian, 'they've brought the piano.'

Caterina could do nothing but stare as the group appeared

with the instrument and say, in Italian, 'Bring it in.' As the five men hauled the magnificent new piano into the room, Caterina circled them, offering comments in Italian: 'Good, ahh, it's lovely, I've been waiting for it, put it there.' For some reason, maybe to involve Joe who sat down on the floor to watch the goings-on, she switched to English. 'I feel so guilty when I move,' she said, but she was addressing the workmen who puffed and strained as they adjusted the heavy instrument, 'because I have to get a new piano and they're so heavy, *si?*' and she was back into Italian. 'Heavy, no?' The workmen placed the piano where she wanted it, and unloosed the broad straps they'd used to carry it in. Caterina moved around it, making certain it was where it should be, and found herself by the kicked-in television set. The maid was looking at her and Caterina told her to bring a broom.

One of the workmen looked at what she meant and saw the set. 'Take a look at this,' he said to his pals in Italian.

'It just blew up,' Caterina said innocently in Italian, 'like a bomb. Do you want it?'

'What'll I do with it?' the man said in Italian.

'It's a present to you from me,' she said.

The man shrugged, and then picked up the set and mumbled something to one of the others about maybe his cousin could get it fixed cheap, and they all trooped out. Concetta appeared with the broom and began to sweep up the mess.

Caterina eyed her nervously, waiting, impatient. Finally, because she had to say something to her son to pick up the thread of what she'd been talking about, she went over to where he sat on the floor. 'When I look at you,' she began, and hesitated. 'When I look at your friends,' she started over, 'it scares me.' She was saying it all wrong and turned abruptly away from him and closed her eyes. 'Oh God,' she uttered softly, 'I feel like I'm on Mars.'

The maid finished sweeping and made for the door, saying over her shoulder in Italian, 'I'm finished.'

Caterina stared at the door as it closed, leaving her finally alone with Joe. When she began talking, she still didn't turn to look at him. 'Maybe it's because you're all unhappy,' she said, 'or spoiled, or neurotic.' That made her look in his direction. He sat on the floor, looking down at the carpet, fiddling with the cuff of his jeans. 'I don't know,' she admitted. 'I don't think it's touching, I think it's awful.' Joe looked up, saying nothing. 'Do you seem different to me because you're really different, or is it just because you're young and maybe my mother would have felt the same way?' She'd pushed herself into questions that were far from what she really wanted to talk to Joe about, and she paused for a moment, to collect her thoughts. She noticed his eyes on her, the indifference burning there. 'Am I boring you?' she asked him. 'Do you understand anything? I come from a world where singing, dreaming, creating, mean something—' and again she had to pause because she'd remembered something, about herself, and about Joe, her only son. 'Jesus,' she said, feeling wretched, 'do you know how long it's been since you told me one of your dreams?'

Joe got to his feet and went over to the newly delivered piano and sat down. He stared at his mother until her eyes met his, and then began to beat out a three-chord riff, the one kids play when they get together to play 'Heart and Soul', or 'Blue Moon'. He began to sing, but without using words: *'Ba-daam baam baam baam, ba-daam baam baam baam—'* He stopped abruptly, looked over at her, and said, 'You sing.'

Concetta, out in the garden, heard the piano playing, the happy beat, heard Joe trying to sing, and then heard Caterina humming along, humming the melody to 'Blue Moon'. Crazy Americans, she thought to herself, one minute they're depressed and two seconds later they're singing and feeling terrific. Shaking her head philosophically she went off to the kitchen to prepare supper.

But Caterina was not singing 'Blue Moon'. She was humming the melody, and as she moved to sit next to Joe on the piano bench she was saying, 'Joey, Joey,' to the tune. She made herself smile and he looked back at her with a tight happy grin as he continued to bang out the chord progressions. 'Joey, Joey, Joey . . . Happy Birthday . . .' She moved her hand on his wrist, and then slowly moved it up the arm. She was still smiling, but her eyes were riveted to his arm, to the crook in the elbow, to that place where—

He suddenly stopped playing and caught her hand as it moved on his arm. Her eyes rose and met his. 'Show me,' she said quietly, with determination, and saw the uncertainty in his eyes, as if he hadn't understood where she was leading. 'Yes,' she added.

He pulled away from her and stood up, frightened. 'Fuck off.'

Caterina's anger boiled over and she couldn't stop herself and she cried out, 'Bastard!' and grabbed for him.

Joe pulled free and then stood, facing her. 'Come on,' he dared her. 'You want to fight? You fucking bitch! You bitch.'

They leaped at one another, almost as if on signal. Joe swung at her as she turned and kicked at him. He grabbed one of her hands and twisted. She pulled away and again caught at his arms. 'Show me,' she insisted, enraged. 'Show me!'

'No!' he cried, and swung again.

She shoved him violently, knocking him off balance. 'Show me.'

'Fuck off!' he yelled, and pulled and then swung and hit her in the side. She swung back and caught him across the head. He staggered, and began to flail at her blindly, wanting to do more than punch her, wanting to hurt her.

'You bastard,' she said through gritted teeth, and hit him again, harder, raising her arm to ward off his blows.

'Fuck you, bitch!' he cried, and swung again. 'Fucking bitch! You bitch! Fucking asshole!'

She ducked as he swung at her again and then she kicked him, made him lose his balance, and hit him again as he raised one hand to stop her blow and then swung with his other hand and caught her hard across the head. Staggered, she fell back against the wall, letting go of him.

'I hate you,' he cried, and started off towards his room. 'You bitch . . .'

Caterina sagged where she stood, fighting for breath. Her hair was matted across her face, which was soaked in perspiration. Her eyes, wide with terror, seemed to see nothing. She reached out to find the sofa, and slowly collapsed on to it, breathing hoarsely, gulping the air hungrily.

Joe came into his room, a smaller version of the living room, a smaller studio-like space which had been fixed up for him with a bunk bed on the floor, tape deck behind it, and posters on the wall: baseball players (Yankees), rock stars, action stills, and a gigantic map stretched across the wall behind the back of his bed. He got himself a glass of water from a cooler he had, and then threw some of it on his face. He took off his shirt, and then pulled his belt out of his pants. He shoved the small table by the bed to one side and saw the book lying under it. He opened it until he came to the page where he'd stashed the 'lid' of 'H'. He got it out, and then grabbed the plastic pencil holder in which he kept his works. Working swiftly and surely he got out the spike and spoon, wet the cotton with some of the alcohol he had, and prepared to cook up the heroin.

Moments later, finished, he rose and crossed to the double doors of his room, which looked out into the small inner garden. He could look across into the living room. Caterina sat on the sofa, unmoving. He turned and went over to the record player and turned it on.

When she heard the music, recognized it as one of her own performances, she managed to get to her feet and walked shakily out into the small garden. She crossed to Joe's doors and called out, 'Joe, would you turn that down?' There was no answer. She knocked and repeated, 'Joe?'

She didn't see him through the doors, standing by his own door, which led out to the main hall and out of the apartment. He saw her reach for the handle of the glass doors, and as she opened it and came into his bedroom he stepped out of it.

'Joe,' he heard her calling. 'Joe?'

He was at the front door, opening it, when he heard the music stop, and in the silence which followed she called to him one last time.

'Joe?'

SIX

The first thing Joe noticed about the Madonna being drawn on the sidewalk by the pavement artist was that the eyes seemed to be following him wherever he went. 'Stop looking at me,' he said, and then crouched to get a better look.

The artist, working in chalk, deftly filled in the spaces around the Madonna's face, and then glanced over at Joe and gave him a nod. Some passersby dropped money into the open box sitting nearby. When Joe saw a dollar bill flutter into it he looked up with a scowl. 'How long do you think it takes him?' an American was saying to his wife.

'Less time than it takes you to mow the lawn,' his wife answered with a smug smile.

The artist saw Joe watching the way he worked with the chalks, and unexpectedly held out his hand, offering the chalk there to Joe. 'You want it?' he asked pleasantly in Italian.

'Oh,' Joe said, momentarily surprised by the offer, and then reached out and accepted the piece of chalk. 'Thank you.'

He looked at the white piece of chalk in his hand and experimentally made a mark on the sidewalk. Pleased, he set off, and when he came to the wall of the first building along his path, he reached out and made his mark, a line that moved with him as he left a trail.

Caterina, meanwhile, was in her car, driving around, uncertain where she would look for Joe first. She remembered him being greeted by friends hanging around the Piazza Farnese and decided to look there. She came into the impressive square and drove over to one of the two magnificent granite bowl fountains dominating the open space and parked. The Piazza was very crowded, as always, and as always the teenagers had made a space for themselves, forcing tourists and Romans to move around them as they tossed their frisbees back and forth.

Caterina recognized a couple of Joe's birthday guests grouped around an ice-cream counter, and started over towards them. A baseball bounced by and Scott, whom she also recognized, chased it. 'Scott,' Caterina called, and he turned and recognized her. 'Have you seen Joe?'

'No,' he said, 'I haven't.' He picked up the ball and tossed it back to another kid Caterina didn't know.

She walked towards the ice-cream counter as Michelle came away from it. 'Where's Joe?' she asked the girl.

'I don't know,' she answered with a shrug and took a lick of the ice cream. She had a particularly unconcerned air about her as she looked around absently at her friends flipping the frisbee back and forth. 'I guess he'll be here soon. I don't know.'

Caterina went over and sat down on one of the stone benches. She looked more carefully at the young people nearby, as if something special might reveal itself to her, some clue to Joe. She saw nothing, and felt a crushing solitude.

Joe's white chalk line ran along the walls of many buildings until it was swallowed up by the shadows of a courtyard full of garbage cans and shiny puddles. It was dark in the courtyard, but the white line ran on and on, into what seemed to be complete darkness.

A ten-year-old street kid, small and dark, appeared at the side of the courtyard and started across it, bobbing his head. He had an empty bottle in his hand and was singing a song in a local neighbourhood dialect: *'I'm the San Lorenzo monster . . . Today, I'm gonna kill you . . . tomorrow, I'll think about ya . . . I'm the—'* He stopped abruptly as his eyes spotted the white line running along the wall of his courtyard. This was his neighbourhood, he was across this yard hundreds of times every day, and the last time through there was no line. What was going on? Curious, he followed it, into the darkness. He went down a few steps, moving cautiously and slowed, and then squatted down and peered through the railings.

Joe was crouched just below the kid, and didn't see the small eyes watching him because he had his belt wound tightly around his upper arm and was concentrating on the needle slipping slowly into the pumped up vein in the crook of his arm. He stifled a small cry and then carefully pushed on the hypo. He wanted to ease the shit into himself, glide it in, let the hit come with a sudden heat that'd last and last for ever. He closed his eyes and his breathing quickened. He knew, he felt shoot through him with a burning wet jolt, the smack snake up through him like fire, into his brain. He relaxed and managed to get his eyes open to carefully pull out the spike. Then he settled back and smiled like an angel.

Something made Joe raise his head and turn. He opened his eyes, and stared at the watching eyes. He rose quickly, fear trying to get through to him as he moved to the far end of the dank basement. He settled there, collapsed against the wall, and continued to breathe heavily, watching his watcher.

A kid! Joe thought to himself as the ten-year-old came into view, grinning amiably, saying, 'I thought you was feeling punk,' in his curious dialect. 'Who taught you the business with the needle?'

Joe didn't know what the fuck he was talking about, and who cared, anyway. There was something else he wanted to talk about, something serious. 'Do you know what happened today?' he said. The kid cocked his head and looked like he knew what Joe was saying. 'Billy Martin left the Yankees. Retired.' Joe nodded. It was heavy news, only now did he appreciate what it meant to him. 'He was one of the greatest Yankee managers since Casey Stengel. God, he was great.' The notion overwhelmed him, how good Billy Martin was. I mean, did anyone know how really good he was? 'He led the Yankees to two championships and one world championship.' His eyes seemed to find the kid, who still watched and listened, the same stupid look on his face. 'You know baseball?' Joe asked him, and shook his head. 'Aw, what do you know? All you guys do is play soccer. You wouldn't understand. He was great.' A sadness filled Joe and made him choke up. 'I don't know why he left,' he said sadly. 'I don't know.' He looked forlornly at the kid. 'Why'd he have to leave?'

Joe got to his feet, stood unsteadily looking around, and then headed back across the basement. The kid fell in by his side. Joe stumbled and caught himself on the wall. He climbed the steps and had to stop because he didn't know where he was. His companion grinned again and raced ahead to a big gate which he swung open. Joe saw light at the end of the corridor and started to run for it, swaying from side to side.

The sun was setting when he came out of the darkness, up the stairs into a small side street. Pale light filled the spaces between the buildings, a roseate wash darkened with blue. Joe stopped to catch his breath. He was sweating now and leaned against a building. The kid caught up to him and then went and leaned against the opposite wall. 'Never seen you roun' here,' he said in his lingo. 'What'ya doin' here?'

Joe heard the question in the kid's voice and said, 'I'm looking for someone.'

'Christ,' the kid cursed, 'he don' unnderstan'!'

Joe had to close his eyes and leaned his head against the cool wet wall. '*Io cercare*,' he said in halting Italian. 'I'm looking . . .'

'Hey,' the kid answered in his dialect, happy to hear Joe say something he understood. But then he shook his head and a knowing look crossed his face. 'You ain't gonna find him in Rome, whoever it is . . .'

Joe pushed away from the wall and started down the small street, moving quickly. The kid trotted alongside.

'I know who ye'r lookin' for,' he said, and took Joe's hand to lead him. They rounded a corner and stopped before a pile of boxes. 'Here he is!' the kid announced and pulled back one of the boxes to reveal a wheezing beggar, his legs pulled up in a foetal position, sleeping. 'Hey, the guy's sleepin'. Looks like yer brother, don't he! Always sleepin'. Eats, and sleeps.' The bum stirred and raised a hand protectively even before his eyes opened to look around. 'Hey,' the kid addressed him. 'Whattaya like? Ya like vino?'

'Pasta, 'n beans,' the bum mumbled, showing a few black teeth and scarred gums. His lips were dry and crusted and his face was streaked with grime. Joe made a face. 'Garlic,' the bum was muttering in Italian, 'oil . . . parsley . . .'

Joe didn't know what the guy was talking about and when the kid suddenly exclaimed and clapped a hand to his forehead like a wizened old man, Joe couldn't understand what had happened. 'Jeez!' the kid cried in dialect, 'the oil! My old lady's out of it, I'm supposed to be gettin' some!' He turned, and dashed off on his skinny legs.

'Wait!' Joe called after him. 'Where you going?'

'Aoh,' someone called out and Joe turned. A man stood in the doorway of a tiny bar. '*Vieni qua,*' he said and gestured for Joe to come over. Without waiting, he turned and went into the bar.

Joe hesitated and then followed him. He didn't know what was going on, and when he came into the small bar the man gestured to the bartender and in Italian said, 'Two cold beers.'

Joe looked around. The place was small, big enough to accommodate a real bar. There was a television set sitting on a shelf. Behind Joe, there was a jukebox, and two tables were set up, to give the impression of a regular kind of place. Joe examined it, and could hear Caterina give it a look and announce, 'This joint's really tacky, dear. What in God's name are you doing here?' He saw the barman take out two frosted bottles and shook his head. 'I don't want a beer,' he said. 'I want an ice-cream cone.'

He turned to the man who had ordered the beers. He was of medium height, with a young, tanned face but old, deep-set eyes and a worn look about him. His clothes were neat, but frayed-looking. As Joe looked at him the man unconsciously ran a hand along his thinning hair. 'Ice cream,' Joe repeated. 'Chocolate ice cream.'

'You are American,' the barman said, like it was an announcement. Joe looked back at him. 'I used to be barman in New York,' he said with a strong accent, pronouncing it 'yewzed'.

'Hey,' Joe said, brightening, feeling relief, and grinned. 'I'm from New York, too. From Brooklyn!' He didn't know why, but he felt excited to see someone who knew New York.

'I used to make drink,' the barman said, 'cocktail, manhattan —' and made a shaking motion with his hands to show how he used to shake up drinks. '*Chuck-chuck* . . .' He put away one of the beers, opened the other one, poured it into a glass, and put it on the bar. The man next to Joe took it as the barman got Joe an ice cream. The man turned and went over and sat down at one of the tables. Joe followed him and sat down opposite.

'So,' the man said in Italian, 'let's talk a little.' He took a sip of his beer and wiped his lips with the back of his hand. He gave Joe a small smile and for a second his gaze seemed to waver uncertainly.

'What?' Joe said, not understanding what the man had said.

'Tell me all about yourself,' the man went on in Italian, and leaned closer, not understanding why Joe wasn't answering him. 'Why aren't you saying anything? I'm listening, you know.'

'*E Americano*,' the barman said to explain Joe's reaction.

The man gave a little shrug and considered Joe. Someone put some money into the jukebox and a moment later a Bee Gees' song from *Saturday Night Fever* began to play. Joe got to his feet, did a few steps, and then handed the man his ice-cream cone and began to dance in earnest. It was a broad, sincere imitation of John Travolta doing his Saturday Night best. Joe jabbed his fingers at sky and floor, did hip-hopped little jerky movements to one side and then the other, and crossed the floor in wide, aggressive steps. It was loose, it was unprofessional, and it looked good.

The man stuck the ice-cream cone into his beer bottle and rose, and as Joe came by him he reached out, and grabbed him in a sudden fierce hug. 'Let's dance,' he said in Italian, 'but the old-fashioned way, like a man and a woman—' he tightened his hold on Joe even as one arm moved around across Joe's back. He held Joe close to him and moved to the rhythm. 'How do you say it in English? "Cheeka-to-cheeka?"'

Joe was suddenly exhausted, and the moment the man's arms held him he half collapsed on the shoulder. 'I'm looking for someone,' he mumbled.

'Whaaa?' the man said, uncertain.

Joe felt even more tired, and as the man made him move back and forth in the dance step, he said, 'I don't know where to find him.'

'Who can understand you,' the man said and looked over at the barman, who was watching them with a bemused expression on his face.

Joe slowly pulled away from the man, eyes not focussing. 'I'm tired,' he mumbled, and turned to look for the table where he had been sitting, adding, in Italian, '*stanco.*' He found the chair, and collapsed into it.

A moment later, he was asleep, his head resting on his arm, a beatific look on his face, which was suddenly transformed, and in sleep made him look like a very little boy.

The man sat back down at the table and stared at the sleeping boy. He was tempted to reach out and touch Joe's hair, but resisted, and instead glanced over at the barman and in Italian said, 'You ever see a Roman fall asleep smiling?' He couldn't help himself, and gently touched Joe's hair. 'Look,' he said quietly, 'look at his beautiful American hair.'

SEVEN

The horizon where sky met sea was a hard pink. Caterina drove along the seaside road, her car whipping past the villas and gardens. She slowed when she came to curves, she could hear the sea out of her open window. Then she would speed up again and the wind blotted out any sounds from outside.

She drove as if uncertain where she wanted to go and why she had come to this place. Her eyes were straining to search out the spaces in the distance even as they swept towards her: another villa, an open stretch of dune, a sudden glimpse of sea, its colour gone a hard metallic grey. She seemed to be lost, yet she drove with an automatic confidence, her hands on the wheel guiding her as if on their own. She turned as a lane passed, and wondered where that lane led.

Then she recognized the house, and slowed down. Yes, it was the house, exactly where she knew it should be. There were the two dunes before the house itself, and the fence with the small garden at the back. There was the varanda, and the rise of beach leading up to it from behind. She pulled over on to the shoulder of the road, on to the firm sand there, and coasted along until she was a short distance from the house itself. Then she turned off the engine and sat staring.

The place looked deserted. She listened, and the lapping of small waves on the shore came to her faintly from beyond the dunes. There was an uninhabited air to her surroundings. She opened the door and stepped out of the car. She suppressed a shiver, and her uncertainty grew inside her and again she asked herself why she'd brought herself to this place; she'd never thought to come here before. It had been so long.

She looked around, and slowly, very slowly, quite unexpectedly, the house before her, the dark sea beyond it, grew familiar. She heard sounds she knew from another time, and the sea air came to her and she could smell its freshness. The veranda became completely familiar to her and suddenly she thought she could hear a piano playing. It was eerie, this moment, because as she heard the music she felt herself sway, slightly, and remembered herself dancing to similar music. But this was a dream. It had to be.

And then she thought she saw a figure appear on the veranda, a tall, terribly familiar figure, and she couldn't help herself. She raised a hand, and before she could stop herself she cried out, 'Giuseppe!'

The music stopped, suddenly. Caterina turned and opened the car door and got back inside. She didn't know if she'd been hearing things and seeing things. She started the engine as the figure of a woman appeared on the veranda. The woman came to the railing and peered into the growing gloom of the evening. Caterina barely glanced at her. She was twisting the wheel, and then gunned the engine and the car took off with a sharp jump, turned completely until it faced back in the direction from which it had come, and sped off.

Back in the bar, it was late when Joe opened his eyes and sat up. He didn't know how much time might have passed. Outside, it was night. He looked over at the bar and saw that the television set above it had been turned on. It looked like a news programme because the picture moved jerkily and there were cops and reporters pushing in and out of the frame and flashbulbs were going off and people were yelling stuff back and forth that Joe associated with news shows. He watched as the camera moved to show someone's body, covered with a canvas. Then the camera panned around to show that the body had been found in a miserable place, squalid and grubby. Joe saw something that looked like crumbling barracks in the background, and then the camera moved again and he could see the sea.

The commentator was talking all the while, in Italian. Joe couldn't understand him as he said: '. . . the investigation of the tragic death of the poet has just started. One point still unclear is whether the young boy being held under suspicion of committing the murder acted alone or with others.'

A small group stood around the bar watching. The man who'd been sitting with Joe was there, too. Joe got up and walked over to the bar. The man turned and saw him. There were tears in his eyes as he stared at Joe for a moment, and then went back to the table where they'd been sitting and sat down. He had a vacant look on his face. Joe didn't realize he was in shock. His eyes rose and once more he was staring at Joe, who turned and looked back at the television set. The body was being picked up by policemen and men who looked like soldiers, from their uniforms, and was carried to an ambulance. The Italian newscast was still going on: 'The initial theory seems unlikely. The body of the famous poet appears to have been—' Joe turned and looked at the man sitting at the table.

He gave a slow sad shake of his head. Joe went back and joined him at the table. The man looked up at him and in Italian said, 'What's your name?'

Joe couldn't understand, and shrugged.

The man looked at him a moment, and then said, 'Do you know what happened?'

Again, all Joe could do was give an apologetic smile and another shrug.

The newscast ended. The barman turned off the set and the few other people either left the place or moved along the bar and picked up their drinks. 'Don't you know? the man asked Joe again in Italian, and then looked over at the barman. 'You explain it, you tell him.'

Joe looked from the man over at the barman, who said, in his broken English, 'They kill this man.' He jerked his thumb over his shoulder at the darkened television set. Joe looked from the set back at the man sitting with him and the man slowly nodded.

'Did you know him?' Joe asked.

'*Si*,' the barman answered for the man and then translated what Joe had asked.

'No,' the man said and shook his head.

'Why'd they kill him?' Joe asked and looked from the man back at the barman.

'*Perchè l'hanno ucciso*?' the barman translated.

'*Perchè era un poeta,*' the man with Joe said quietly.

'*No,*' the barman answered without translating for Joe, '*perchè era un frocio, sai.*'

'*No,*' the man with Joe said with a considered shake of his head.

'*Ma si,*' the barman disagreed.

'*Era un poeta,*' the man repeated, and Joe could hear the insistence in his voice.

'What are you guys talking about?' he said.

'He say he was poet,' the barman said, indicating the man at the table, 'but kill him not because poet but because homosexual.' He looked at the man who listened, his expression empty, and in Italian added, '*Era un poeta, ma l'hanno ammazzato perchè era un frocio.*'

The man turned to Joe and with a look of fierce pain in his eyes declared, '*Qui da noi li* – here in our country they kill poets, you know? Do they do that in America, kill you because you're a faggot?'

Joe once more hadn't understood, and looked to the barman for help. 'Homosexual,' the barman qualified.

Joe looked over as the man nodded, the anger burning in his eyes, yet his look powerfully sad. He leaned closer to Joe, and reached out and began to caress Joe on the bare arm. 'You know,' he said in Italian, speaking very pleasantly, 'you're really pretty.'

Joe yanked his hand away as the barman said, '*Lascia stare . . .*'

The barman had told him to leave Joe alone, but the man went on, in Italian, though his eyes held on Joe. 'Isn't he pretty?' He reached out suddenly and grabbed Joe tightly at the wrist and pulled at him. 'Yes,' he said with bitterness, 'a young kid killed him, a kid about your age.' He tightened his hold, staring at Joe, his anger remorseless. 'Who knows if he was as beautiful as you?' His expression suddenly changed again and became sweet and benign. 'You're truly beautiful,' he almost whispered.

'Let me go!' Joe cried, and desperately tried to get free. The man suddenly let go and Joe pulled back violently. He jumped to his feet and knocked over his chair as he backed away. Then he turned, and ran out of the bar.

The man realized people were watching him. He gestured hopelessly and added a small shrug. '*Ma,*' he said in Italian, 'I didn't do a thing to him.'

Caterina parked the car and almost forgot to lock it. She ran up the steps and into the courtyard of her building and crossed the courtyard to her door.

She fumbled with the keys, found the right one, opened the front door, and ran into the foyer and across it to Joe's room. She was out of breath as she opened it, and as she slowed to catch her breath she stepped in and saw that the room was deserted. She leaned against the door for a moment, fighting to slow her breathing, and then pushed herself away and turned and walked back down the hall.

She came into the kitchen and found the maid, Concetta, sitting at the kitchen table, her head in her arms, asleep. Caterina came over to her and saw that she'd been shelling peas. The bowl of fresh peas was in her lap, the empty sheels on a piece of newspaper laid out on the floor by her chair. 'Concetta,' Caterina said, prodding her gently. 'Concetta.' Concetta opened her eyes and stared sleepily at Caterina. 'Concetta,' Caterina went on in Italian, 'I want you to go away. Right now.'

'What?' the maid answered, confused. She sat up, and made a face as she felt stiffness in her back from having fallen asleep in such an uncomfortable position.

Caterina nodded as she said, 'I'll let you know when you can come back.'

'What have I done?' the poor woman said unhappily.

'You didn't do anything,' Caterina said kindly. 'I want to be alone for a few days.' She took Concetta under the arm and when she'd put the bowl of peas on the table, helped her to her feet.

'Where'm I going to go?' she asked.

Caterina took out some money from her purse and held it out. 'Have you ever stayed in a hotel?' she asked. 'It's fantastic.'

Concetta took the money and stared at it for a moment. She folded it and shoved it into her dress under her apron. Then she untied the apron and laid it over the back of the chair. She started for the door, and then stopped and looked around at the kitchen. 'Don't you want me to clean this up a little?'

'I'll do it,' Caterina said. 'You go. Go, go, go, go!' She shooed Concetta out of the door and closed it behind her.

Alone, Caterina realized it was cold in the kitchen. She suppressed a small shiver, and went to her room to fetch a shawl. She slowed to stare at the small package still on her bed, wrapped prettily, with her card on it. 'For Joe,' it said. It was her birthday present to him. She wrapped the shawl around herself, turned off the lights, and went into the living room. She still felt a bit cold and went over to close the doors leading out into the small garden. She reached for the door handle, and gave a start.

Joe stood before her, swaying unsteadily. She gave a short exclamation. He took a step forward, and collapsed wordlessly into her arms. She helped him sit down. He was very pale, and his forehead was wet with perspiration. He looked up at her, and then away, into empty space. 'I really miss Dad,' he said quietly. She saw him shudder, and he looked back at her. He was shaking, and clutched himself to keep warm. 'Mom,' he cried out in the voice of a frightened and sick child. 'I'm cold.'

'Joey,' she said to him and opened her shawl to wrap him in it. She helped him to his feet, saying, 'Come on. I'll put you to bed right away.' He managed to stand and they started across towards his bedroom. 'You'll have a good sleep,' she comforted him. He stumbled as they got to his doorstep. 'Two steps,' she told him and took a firmer grip on him. 'Come on.'

He took one step and then the other. 'That's a good boy.' She shoved the door open with her elbow and got him across the room to his bed. He collapsed on to it. She slipped off his shoes and unbuckled his belt and started to pull off his jeans. 'Joey,' she said to him so he could help her get the pants off. He lifted himself enough and she slipped them all the way off. She put them over a chair and then turned back to him. 'I don't remember buying you those sexy underpants,' she observed, not knowing if her tone was friendly, or frightened.

'I bought them,' he answered weakly.

She could see how terribly pale he was, and wondered if he was going to throw up. She forced herself to smile, to keep her voice calm. 'Where?' she asked.

'Somewhere in the Piazza di Spagna.' He pushed himself up and somehow got himself to his feet. 'I have to go to the bathroom,' he said, and wobbled to the bathroom and went inside.

Several moments later she heard him cry, 'Fuck. I can't pee.'

She got up and went into the bathroom where he stood, supporting himself on the wall behind the toilet. 'I'll help you,' she said. She put her arms around him to help him stand, and slowly tightened her hold on him, as if to impart some mysterious strength to him. 'Remember,' she almost whispered, 'when you were little and you'd wait to pee till you got on my bicycle?' Joe said nothing and she could feel him straining weakly in her arms. She hesitated, but only for a moment, and then reached down to hold his soft penis above the toilet bowl.

He finished quickly and was about to go back into the bedroom when he hiccuped raspily and then coughed. His body heaved and he started to retch, crying out to her in the same moment. She caught him from behind, and suddenly he went slack in her arms and lost consciousness.

Caterina stood for a terrible moment, holding him, afraid he might fall, and then she began to drag him, out of the bathroom across the bedroom towards his bed. 'Oh, God,' she whispered in terror. 'Oh, God, oh, God, oh, God . . .'

By the time the doctor came to examine him, Joe was in a deep sleep. Caterina watched the man probe the boy's body and lift each eyelid to shine a small light into the pupils. When he was finishing, she said, 'How long is he going to sleep?'

'Three or four months,' the doctor answered, speaking in a thick accent. He looked at her with a professional eye, and clicked his bag shut.

'No,' Caterina said as the doctor got to his feet, 'sleep.'

'When he wakes up,' the doctor said, 'he will feel weak.' He walked across the room to the bedroom door and turned. 'He will be very hungry. Give him something to eat and talk to him.' His expression grew more serious and he said nothing for a moment, as if considering precisely the words he wished to use. 'Talk to him a lot,' he finally said.

Caterina looked back over to the sleeping figure and said, 'I'll leave some milk for him, in case he wakes up.'

'He will wake up in about twenty-four hours,' the doctor said.

Caterina accompanied him to the front door of the apartment and opened it for him. He stepped out into the hall and turned back to her. For some strange reason he raised a hand, as if to protest. 'Don't worry,' he declared, 'you owe me nothing.'

This seemed curiously abrupt to Caterina, and she was about to say something when he gestured again, at the same time reaching behind his back with his other hand.

'But,' he went on, 'there is something you can do for me.' Without waiting for her to respond, he whipped a Polaroid camera out from behind him. 'I would like to take a picture of you.'

'A picture!' Caterina exclaimed, and before she could do or say anything more, the flashbulb went off in her face. She didn't know whether to laugh or cry, and could only slowly close the door on him. 'Bye, bye,' she said softly.

She went into te kitchen and poured a glass of milk and took it into Joe's room. She moved a chair next to his bed, put the glass on it, and straightened up. Her son was sleeping soundly, his lips slightly parted, a soft sibilance escaping them every time he exhaled. It was a heavy sleep, deep, far away, and she remembered terrible moments when as a baby he'd been in the grip of a fever and his sleep had been similar, deep and troubled and helpless. That's what she saw as she stood looking down at him: he was helpless.

In the morning, light filled the apartment, poured into all of the rooms through the large windows, and competed with the sound of Caterina exercising which flowed everywhere. She worked on arpeggios and switched to four-note phrases, and then back to the arpeggios.

Joe slept, oblivious to the light and sound around him.

Caterina was wearing leotards under a sweatshirt and exercise shorts. She continued practising at the piano for several moments and abruptly stopped, crying out rather than singing a note. There was a silence, and then she got up and went into the other end of the room, where her exercise equipment was set up. Without hesitating, with no preparation or stretching, she began to do split jumps, doing them faster and faster until sweat filmed her upper lip and brow and she was breathing very hard.

She only stopped when the intercom phone rang. She picked it up. '*Si?*'

'It's me,' she heard Marina's voice say.

'Come in.' Caterina said, and rang the buzzer which would open the front door. A few moments later, when Caterina opened the curtains leading from the exercise room out into the small garden, she saw Marina appear in the opposite doorway and start across. She was wearing a loose shirt over slacks and had her handbag slung over her shoulder. 'Hey,' she said brightly. '*Ciao.*'

'Sh!' Caterina cautioned immmediately. 'Joe's asleep.'

'Asleep?' Marina said, and stepped into the exercise room.

'He's sick,' Caterina said, and resumed doing split jumps.

'Poor thing,' Marina said sympathetically. 'Let me say hello to him.'

'No,' Caterina ordered, and stopped doing jumps. 'Come here.' Marina hesitated, and then came closer. 'Turn around.'

Marina turned slowly. Before she could protest, Caterina

grabbed her, by the arms, and began twisting her one way and then the other in a gruelling exercise designed to stretch the shoulder muscles. 'Ai, ow!' Marina cried, 'what are you doing?' Caterina ignored her protest, and only did it more quickly. 'My mother died of heart attack!' Marina gasped, yanked back and forth, side to side. 'Ah, ah, ah!' she cried, 'you're killing your voice like this.'

Caterina stopped as suddenly as she'd started, dropped to the floor, and said, 'Sit down.'

'What are you trying to do?' Marina asked. When Caterina waved her to the floor, she reluctantly obeyed, sitting opposite Caterina.

'Put your feet here,' Caterina told her and stretched hers apart. Marina pressed her feet against Caterina's, until the two pairs of feet formed a diamond. And then Caterina grabbed Marina's arms and began pulling her back and then pushing her forward.

'You, you,' Marina began to protest, 'you are so goddamned American!' She was being torn apart, yanked by her arms and split wide in the middle. 'You are like John Wayne!' She couldn't get free of Caterina, whose grip was like iron. 'Oh, no, *basta!*' Marina pleaded. '*Basta!*'

And just as suddenly Caterina once again let go, and collapsed back on to the exercise mat. Marina lay for several moments, fighting to catch her breath. Then she pulled herself up alongside Caterina. She could see Caterina's face, her expression strained, driven as if still in the throes of physical exertion. 'Why don't we go away some place for a week?' Marina suggested.

Caterina didn't answer, but slowly pulled herself to her feet, and gave a harsh laugh.

Marina thought Caterina liked the idea, and got up and followed, laughing with her. 'Just, just the two of us,' she continued. 'To Morocco.'

Caterina was still laughing, but there was another sound in her voice, too, as if she had swallowed a sob. She came to the shower, at the end of the exercise area, and opened the door and then began to pull off her clothes.

'What do you think?' Marina asked, watching Caterina pull the sweaty clothes off of herself.

Caterina raised her head momentarily and took a deep, pain-filled breath. 'Oh, God,' she exclaimed to herself. She got into the shower and reached for the water taps.

'You need a lover,' Marina advised her.

Caterina stopped, and turned back to throw Marina a sharp look. '*Cunt*,' she spat out softly, and then turned the water on until it beat heavily down on her body.

Marina was momentarily taken aback by Caterina's response. Then, unable not to, she moved closer, to the shower stall door, until she could look over it. She stared as Caterina soaped herself, raising her head to let the water stream down it. It took Marina a moment to tear her eyes away from the pale pink of Caterina's body and look up into her eyes. There was something inexpressively sad in them; Caterina seemed to be trying to say something.

'I don't want to sing any more,' she said finally.

'Why?' Marina said, as shocked by the remark as by Caterina's hurled insult.

But instead of answering, Caterina burst into helpless weeping. Tears poured down her face, mixing with the water splashing on her body.

'No, Caterina,' Marina said to comfort her, and switched to Italian. '*No, no, non piangere*,' lovingly urging her friend not to cry any more. '*Non piangere*.' Caterina reached out to her, and Marina opened the door and stepped into the running shower and took Caterina into her arms and then collapsed, weeping desperately.

The crying and the water and Marina holding her broke the tension in Caterina. She cried more heavily but less helplessly, and raised her head to stare at Marina. Marina was soaked. Caterina pulled her head back, to see better. She still sobbed, but the sight of Marina covered with water, her clothing ruined, was ludicrous and Caterina started to laugh. Marina met her look and tried to manage a smile. This made Caterina laugh even more, and through her tears she clutched at Marina and laughed helplessly.

EIGHT

Joe still slept. Caterina, wrapped in a blanket, stood watching him. Her hair was still wet from the shower and her eyes were red and puffy. Marina had borrowed some clothes, had changed, and left. Alone now in Joe's room, Caterina leaned against the wall and watched him in his sleep.

His map of the United States was there on the wall behind his bed and she found herself staring at it. The names of cities sprang out, some of the names very familiar, others totally foreign to her. Boston, she thought to herself, I sang there. She glanced down at Joe. Do you remember Boston? she thought. Her eyes returned to the map. Providence, you were a little boy, you learned how to swim. Then we went to Cape Cod, and you'd swim there. I like Boston, she was thinking now. Her eyes began to roam more freely across the giant map, and thoughts came tumbling into her mind:

Hartford. I sang there. Philadelphia, Philadelphia's the best place, really, I think it's the best place in America to sing. But you didn't come with me. You were little. Detroit – her eye had caught another name – Detroit! is the worst place in America, God, I hate Detroit! I hope I never have to sing in Detroit. Oh, Buffalo! I sang there. God, all those lakes! Did you ever go to the Great Lakes with me? Canada. We should go there. I really haven't been to Canada. I took a train, once, all the way across the country, through the mountains . . . So many mountains in America, all the way over to San Francisco. God, that's a beautiful place. Mountains, desert, valleys, ocean. All is so wild. I've never been there. We should go to the mountains. We should get horses and go riding. Take a summer off and just go into the mountains. San Francisco. I love singing in San Francisco. It's like singing in Europe . . .

Her thoughts faltered, as if she'd tripped herself up. She

turned and stared back at her beloved sleeping son. 'Joe,' she said very softly. 'I don't want to sing any more.'

She moved away from the wall, and went over to where Joe's clothes lay on the floor. She took the blanket off, and picked up Joe's jeans and put them on. She fastened the belt, and then picked up his shirt, and put it on.

When she was dressed she examined herself in a mirror. She didn't know why she was doing this, but knew she felt compelled. It frightened her, and she turned and gave Joe another look. Then she left his room, closing the door very quietly behind her.

Once in her car and driving, Caterina felt less aimless even though she wasn't sure where she was going. She touched the collar of Joe's shirt and inhaled, smelling him, that still boyish scent of soap and young sweat.

She got to the Piazza Farnese, parked the car, and got out. She was barefoot, and without any make-up she looked like a teenager. No one would have recognized Caterina Silveri. She looked around. There were very few people there. A group of tourists were heading across towards the Farnese Palace. Their guide was pointing to the palace's upper floors and Caterina heard him say something about, 'Michelangelo . . .' Caterina went over to where the kids had been buying ice cream. The counter was deserted. She raised her hand to shield her eyes from the bright sun and looked around again. The place seemed deserted. Disappointed, she went back to her car.

She opened the door to get in and stopped short. The boy she'd seen greet Joe, the one with the dark skin and the large black eyes and tightly curled hair was sitting in the front seat. 'Who are you?' she said, and added, '*Chi e*?'

'I am Mustafa,' he introduced himself in English.

'You're Joe's friend?'

'Yes,' he acknowledged with a pretty little nod.

'What do you want?' Caterina asked.

'I was thinking to steal your car,' he answered, a playful look on his face.

'I want to talk to you,' Caterina said.

'Not here,' Mustafa stopped her. 'No, not here. At my house.' He got out of the car. 'Follow me.'

He went over to his motorscooter and got on it. When he took off, she followed, through narrow streets, until they entered Rome's Casbah, an area that looked like the most squalid of North African villages. There were hovels abutted against the large shabby buildings. Gypsies wandered around in the narrow dirt roads, most carrying tiny babies that all seemed to Caterina to be wailing furiously. Caterina held close to her guide as he scurried past the people who eyed her contemptuously. When he swung sharply into a dark doorway she almost missed him and went past. A hand reached out and caught her to steer her back. 'Take the stairs,' he told her and pointed.

She followed him up a narrow flight of stairs that turned round and round, going higher not into light but gloom. When they found themselves before a door, Mustafa felt around until he found a bunch of keys, and took it out. He selected one, opened the doors, and went in. Caterina hesitated, and then followed. 'Lock well the door,' he called after her.

The room she entered was poorly lit and for the first few moments she was more aware of the way the place felt rather than the way it looked. There was something sweet and oppressive in the air and then she recognized the smell of stale incense. When her eyes accustomed to the light she looked around. Someone, she guessed it was Mustafa, had tried to give the room an 'Arab' look. There was a large mat in the middle of the floor, with pillows thrown around it. There were a few cushions as well, and two low tables. One of the walls had a worn throw tacked up.

Mustafa saw her examining the room and said, 'Beautiful, no?' He gestured hospitably. 'Please, sit down.' Caterina looked around. 'I prepare you mint tea, Arab style, best you ever try.' Before she could answer, he disappeared behind a curtain.

Caterina went over and sat down one of the cushions. She

looked around, and then at the walls by her head. There were cut-out pornographic photographs pinned up of naked women, their legs spread wide, their hands spreading themselves even wider. Next to these were photographs of simple Arab scenes, women at wells, children in villages playing. Caterina looked away and sniffed the air. There was some scent there and she wondered if it might be more stale incense. Crazy images of smoky Arab dens flooded into her mind and she shook them quickly away.

'Forget,' she began to say, and found it difficult to speak, 'forget your Arab tea. Do you sell that stuff to my son?' Mustafa didn't answer, as if he hadn't heard.

She got up and went over to the curtain and pulled it aside just as he was dropping a jellaba over his shoulders. She caught a glimpse of brown naked skin, and then he pushed his head up through it, and turned to give her a grin. Embarrassed, she dropped the curtain and went back to where she had been sitting. She'd seen the thin matttress lying there on the floor, and realized it was where he slept.

When he reappeared, he was carrying a small teapot and a can. He went over to a small stove and busied himself pouring out water and then measuring out spoonfuls of tea. He worked with care, deliberate and methodical, looking up once to see if she possibly appreciated the attention he was paying to pleasing her.

'Do you sell it to him?' Caterina asked him once more, and then, angered, repeated it more sharply. 'Do you? Answer me.'

Mustafa put the leaves into the water, covered it, and then turned. 'Sit down,' he said and brought the teapot and two cups to the small table nearest her.

Something in his manner, something imperious and knowing, unsettled Caterina and threw her into a more helpless state of mind. She watched him carefully pour hot water into the teapot, and decided to sit down. 'Why do you do it?' she said.

Mustafa's eyes rose from where he was adjusting the teapot

and looked at her with childish wisdom. 'I must eat,' he declared.

'Oh, bullshit!' Caterina said and lost her temper. 'That's really an excuse. I can't stand people who say that.' She felt relief that he'd got her angry again. 'Why don't you go get a job?' she suggested testily, and pointed a finger at him. 'You don't get a job because you hate work.'

'Listen,' Mustafa said calmly, and made himself comfortable on one of the cushions. 'My village is near the desert. When I was fifteen, I was sold to a rich Italian.' He paused as the tea finished steeping, and then poured out two cups, picked up one, and held it out to her. She took it, but did not try it.

'Then the Italian got tired of me, and threw me out. I was without a place to sleep and nothing to eat. Do you really believe I haven't looked for work?' he asked her.

When she didn't react, and said nothing, he suddenly grinned. 'You're right,' he admitted. 'I hate to work, when there is no work.'

His argument confused her, and she decided to say nothing for the moment. She moved the cup to her lips, cautious not to burn herself. When she tasted it, the mint was there, on her tongue and lips. She tried another sip, and then politely put the cup down and said, 'Do you have anything stronger I could put in the tea?'

'I'm sorry,' Mustafa said, putting one hand apologetically to his chest. 'My religion does not permit me to drink alcohol.'

'Your *religion*?' She gave a short laugh, turned away, and saw the drawing stuck on the wall. It was a picture of Joe.

'Did you do that?' she said.

'Yes,' Mustafa said. 'He's walking.'

'Yes,' Caterina agreed. 'It's good . . .'

'Do you know where he's going?'

'No,' she said. 'Where?'

'You know,' Mustafa prodded her.

'No,' she insisted. 'I don't. Where? No, Mustafa,' she said again. 'I don't know where he's going.'

'Yes,' he nodded solemnly. 'You're his mother, you know him better than I.'

'I don't know.'

'He's coming here.'

Caterina stared and then looked back at Mustafa. 'Does he come here often?'

'Yes,' Mustafa said. 'Even when he doesn't need to buy. He lies on the bed and talks and talks. We're friends.'

'What does he talk about?' Caterina asked.

'Everything,' Mustafa said. 'You. He's different from the others.'

'Different? What do you mean, different?'

'He's very lonely,' Mustafa answered. He rose and went over to a cupboard and took out a small box and a small set of scales. 'You know that.'

Caterina watched, unable to tear her eyes away, as he began to weigh out a white powder. Each time he had the proper weight he would tip it into a prepared square of paper which he professionally folded over six times to form a precise little packet. 'How much does that cost?'

Mustafa turned and saw her looking at him and then turned back to his work. 'Two hundred thousand lira a gram.'

'What!' she exclaimed. 'You're kidding!' She couldn't help herself and laughed. 'That's more expensive than diamonds, caviar, truffles.' She got up and came over to look at it.

'I only get a small ten per cent,' he said. She reached out and moved the scale. 'Careful,' he cautioned.

She moved back to safety and said, 'Where does Joe get that kind of money?'

Mustafa finished what he was doing, the box and scales were returned to the cupboard, and he turned back to her, his hands hidden in the loose folds of his robe. 'He steals it from you,' he said unemotionally. 'Haven't you noticed?'

'You're Joe's friend, right?'

'I like him very much,' Mustafa told her with a gesture of sincerity.

'You care about him,' Caterina went on, quickly, to what had been taking shape in her mind. 'Let me propose something to you.' She clutched her purse – the timing had to be right, she'd never done anything like this. 'I'll give you a lot of money. Just tell Joe, tell him you don't have any more of this.'

Mustafa stared at her for a moment, a touch of pity in his eyes, and then shook his head. 'Don't worry. I'm closing the shop.' Caterina wasn't sure she understood him, couldn't believe he was saying this. His eyes found hers and he gave her a small smile. 'I've put money aside, for a plane ticket. I'm going back to my country.'

He saw relief flood into her face and he smiled more broadly. 'Happy?' The boldness of the remark made her turn away from him self-consciously. 'Don't blush.'

'Don't talk to me like that,' she said and looked back to him. 'I could be your mother.'

'My mother blush, too,' Mustafa said, and went over and picked up a small photograph. He brought it to Caterina and showed it to her.

She stared at a picture of a small beautiful boy in a woman's arms. The woman had a serene look on her face but it was the baby's eyes which lit up the entire photograph. Upset, Caterina turned away and opened her purse. She dug around in it until she found the billfold and got a roll of bills out of it. Without counting them she shoved them over to Mustafa. 'Take this,' she said.

Mustafa looked at it, and then accepted it with a gracious nod. 'Thank you.' She turned to go but he said, 'Wait, wait,' and reached under the folds of his jellaba and felt around until he found something. 'Here,' he said and pulled out one of the small silvery packets and held it out to her.

Caterina stared at it, dumfounded, and then looked at him, fear in her eyes. 'I don't want it,' she said with horror.

He came very close to her, his gestures careful and kind, and reached out to press the packet into her hand. 'Joe might need it,' he said gently.

There was nothing she could say in answer. She left in silence, holding her purse to her as if fearing someone might discover its terrible contents.

By the time she got home it was dark. She parked, and went up to her front door. She realized she was worn out, exhausted, and for a moment a wish, a small tiny wish crossed her mind. She discarded it, found her key, and opened the door.

The first thing she saw was an enormous bouquet of flowers sitting in a vase on the foyer table. The sight of them momentarily took her breath away. When she approached them, she saw that there was a note attached. '*Lunge da te*,' it said, '*per me non v'ha diletto.*' It was Alfredo's words from *La Traviata*: 'Far from you there's no joy for me.' Caterina whirled and looked around. 'Joe!' she called out, a feeling of incredible relief flooding through her. 'Joe!'

She rushed across into the living room and once more had to stop short because the dining table had been set up and plates and silverware ceremoniously arranged on it, dinner for two, complete with fresh candles in candle holders. 'Joe!' she cried out again, and rushed out of the room, down the hall to the kitchen.

She found him there, wearing nothing but his underpants, bent over a cookbook. The kitchen was in the most incredible disarray she'd ever seen: dirty pots were everywhere, boxes and cartons lying open, flour spilling out of a bag, cracked eggs on the counter and in the sink. The radio was on, blaring out rock and roll, and Joe was carefully spooning something from one bowl into another.

'What are you doing?' she said, incredulous.

Joe looked up, and saw her. 'Oh, hi,' he said cheerfully. There was colour in his cheeks, and his eyes looked at her directly, with the open simplicity she felt she had once known so well.

'You look great!' she exclaimed, and rushed over and threw her arms around him from behind.

'I really had a terrific sleep,' he said. When she moved her head around and started to kiss him on the cheeks, he squirmed away. 'Hey,' he protested, 'lipstick!'

She turned him away from his work and examined him. 'Nope,' she declared.

'Good,' he said and turned back to his bowls. 'I'm preparing you a delicioso dinner.' He picked up the big bowl, and slowly poured the mixture into a soufflé pan sitting on a pot of water which was steaming. Caterina stuck out a finger and caught some of the batter and tasted it. 'Ma!' he protested.

She moved a few feet away, and then came back and leaned over to sniff. 'Good, mmmm.'

'It's a French-style soufflé,' he announced to her, and kneeled to set the timer.

Caterina looked around, and then back at the soufflé in the pot.

'Fancy, huh?' he said.

'Fancy,' she agreed. 'And candlelight, too.'

Joe nodded and glanced at the timer. 'You now have nineteen minutes and forty-five seconds to get dressed.' He looked over at her. 'Where'd you get my clothes?'

Caterina ignored this and was saying, 'Nineteen minutes . . .' She turned and took off out the door, racing across the living room to her own room.

'—and forty-five seconds,' he called after her. He looked around at the kitchen, checking to make sure he hadn't forgotten everything, and then went to his own room and began to get dressed.

It took him a long time – for him – almost fifteen minutes, and he was very nervous about his appearance. He had put on freshly pressed pants, and a clean shirt, a tie, and his new white jacket. He was worried about his hair sticking up in back and kept pushing it down as he paced out in the small garden, waiting for his mother to appear. Every few seconds he would look at the new watch on his wrist, the one she'd given him for his birthday.

'Do you like your present?' he heard her say, and looked up.

The curtains from her bedroom parted and she stood before

him in a stunning gown of layered silks, flowing and loose, moving as if with the gentle breezes that found their way into their small garden.

For a moment the breath caught in his throat, and then he nodded. 'Thank you,' he said, and went over and gave her a small kiss on the cheek. Just then the timer in the kitchen went off loudly and he whirled. 'Oh, my God,' he moaned. 'Oh, shit. The soufflé.' He let go of her and ran out of the garden into the kitchen.

From the moment he got it out of its pan on to a platter, he knew he'd blown it. He almost decided to throw it away, but Caterina was waiting, and he wanted her to see he'd at least tried. She was waiting for him in her place at the table when he brought the platter out and put it in front of his place, ready to be served. He stared at it for a second and then looked up at her. 'God, it looks awful.'

'No, it isn't,' she said.

'It looks like a dead frisbee.' He shoved a big spoon into it and slopped two servings on to the two plates. He handed her one and put the other one in his place.

'It's genius, Joe,' Caterina insisted. 'It's inspiration. It's a masterpiece. I never could have done it. I don't know how you did it.' She took a forkful and paused to consider it. 'Maybe—' she began, but Joe interrupted her.

'Ma,' he said, 'just because you're my mother, you don't have to eat it.'

'Put a little salt on it, darling,' she suggested, salted her own, and passed him the shaker.

Joe shook some salt on the portion before him and then tasted it. Instantly, he spat and threw down his fork. 'It's awful,' he cried. 'It sucks! I fucked it up.' He shoved his plate away from him and sank back in his chair. The supper was a disaster, a real fuck-up.

'Let's have some champagne,' Caterina suggested brightly, 'okay?' She got up and got the bottle out of the ice bucket where it had been chilling. She looked at it and then came over and gave it to Joe. 'Would you open it for us, darling? It scares me.

It's like a missile going off, like an explosion.'

When Joe began to undo the gold wrapping at the bottle's neck she clapped her hands over her ears. 'Tell me when it's over,' she said in a high voice like an excited little girl. 'Tell me when it's over.' She closed her eyes as Joe slowly eased the cork up and up, and she had to look away, genuinely unnerved by the impending pop. 'Is it over, Joe?' she asked without looking.

There was no 'pop' at all. Joe looked at her and then said, 'Pop!' Caterina giggled and uncovered her ears as Joe held the bottle over one of the glasses as foam bubbled up and dribbled down the side of the bottle. She sat back as he came around and filled her glass with the wine and then went back to fill his own. He put the bottle down, picked up his glass, and stared across at his mother.

'To Joe,' she said, and raised her glass to him.

He put down his glass, but his stare stayed on her, direct, and when he spoke, he spoke directly. 'Do you know why I take dope? Because I don't give a shit.'

Caterina had raised her glass, expecting some sort of answer to her toast. She hesitated, and then lowered it to the table with studied care. 'I see,' she said.

'I don't give a shit,' he repeated.

'About what?' she asked, knowing she had to tread carefully. 'What are you talking about?'

'I don't give a shit about anything,' he said.

'Why, Joe?'

When he answered her, there was not a trace of bitterness in his voice and his expression was empty of any emotion. 'I've got nothing to lose,' he said.

Caterina met his level gaze and said, 'Because you've got a mother giving you the money.'

'If I didn't have the money,' he said, 'I'd steal it.'

To conceal her tension, Caterina rose and walked slowly across the room. 'I believe you,' she said before turning to look back at him.

'I need two fixes a day,' he said, and got to his feet.

Caterina didn't know what he was going to do, but if he was

going to take one of those shots now, she wanted to make him understand something first. 'I can't watch you killing yourself,' she said, and it was an admission, selfishly painful to be making, because she was speaking more for herself as a person than as a mother talking to a wayward child.

'If I don't get it,' he said, 'I get sick. I get cramps, I get a cold sweat.' He was speaking more urgently now. 'I shake all over. Then I take a shot and it all goes away. Shooting up makes me feel wonderful.'

His voice had risen as he said the word, *wonderful*, and his expression changed. Worry seemed to disappear and for a moment he was that beautiful-faced boy she loved so fiercely. 'How can I help you?' she asked, terrified of what she was seeing.

'Leave me alone,' he told her. 'What makes you think you can help me? I don't like you helping me.' He jumped up from the table, and hurried out of the room, crying, 'Just leave me alone.'

She sat there for several moments, not knowing what she could possibly do, when there was a terrible cry from his room. 'Oh, God! I don't have any more junk! I'm going to die.'

Seconds later, he came back, but now his gait had changed and he was unsteady on his feet, reaching out to catch himself from falling. 'You didn't like my dinner, did you?' he said helplessly. 'You don't understand anything about me. God, I'm sick. I'm dying.'

'Joe,' Caterina said, and reached blindly for her purse. 'Come here.' She dug around until she found the small silvery packet. 'I can help you, Joe.' She hesitated but for a moment, and then took it out and held it for him to see.

'What?' he said. He was already trembling, andwhen he saw what she had in her hand his expression changed and he was momentarily stunned. 'Where did you get it?' he asked, and carefully took it out of her hand.

'Mustafa.'

'Oh, God,' he uttered softly. 'Thank you.' He rushed over to the dining table and grabbed a spoon and handed it to her.

'Here, hold this.' He carefully opened the small packet and poured the white powder into the spoon. 'Careful,' he cautioned, eyes burning as he watched the powder collect in the shiny scoop. 'Careful.'

Caterina didn't move. When the powder was all out of the packet, he added some water to it and then pulled off his jacket and flung it on the floor and began to roll up his sleeve, always watching the spoon in her hand. 'Take it easy,' he cautioned. When he had his sleeve rolled up he moved her hand, brought it over one of the candles still burning on the table. She held it above the flame and he took her hand again. 'No,' he said and showed her how it was to be done. 'Back and forth.'

Caterina began moving the spoon back and forth over the flame. Her eyes were rivited to the powder, too. When it began to melt, she heard Joe, by her side, sigh. 'That's it.' The powder mixed with the liquid. 'That's it, back and forth,' he whispered, and urgently added, 'Come on . . .' A moment later, and the liquid bubbled. She took it away from the flame and looked at him. 'Thank you,' he said, and then turned and ran out of the room.

She sat holding the spoon, waiting. Suddenly, he reappeared, wild-eyed, shrieking, 'You forgot the needle!' He tore across the room, as if searching for something. 'I'm going to die!' He stopped in front of her and wailed, 'I don't have any more god-damned needles!' He was clutching his bare arm. 'I'm going to die!' Caterina didn't know what to say, and stood, staring at him, the spoon of liquified heroine in her hand. '*You forgot to get a needle!*'

He looked around, completely out of control, and grabbed a fork off the table. Caterina watched, mesmerized, knowing almost by instinct what he was about to do as part of her refused to believe it. She stared as Joe put the fork against his arm, into the pale hollow at the crook of the arm, and shoved, very hard. He gasped, and made himself push harder. The fork dropped from his hand and three tiny holes appeared, followed by three tiny streams of blood.

Caterina screamed and dropped the spoon. She stood for

another terrible moment, and then threw herself on him and began to suck the blood from the wound.

Joe was deathly white; what he had just tried to do had frightened even him. Tears welled up in his eyes and he began to cry. He collapsed into his mother's arms and felt her holding him with all of her strength, enfolding him, protecting him. 'Don't call the doctor,' he was able to murmur. 'Please.' She got to the couch and collapsed with him on to it. He sank to the floor, Caterina with him, swallowing his sobs.

'Oh, God,' she moaned, 'it's all my fault. It's all my fault.' She tenderly kissed his wet cheeks, and then his mouth, repeating, 'it's all my fault.' She continued to kiss him, moving to his tear-streaked face, and his eyes.

'Don't put me to sleep again,' he begged.

'What have I done to you?' she cried.

Joe found her hand and rubbed it over his face, down around his neck, and then moved it to his chest. He pressed it to him, moving it as he himself began to move against it. His eyes were squeezed shut, and he rolled against and then away from her as he continued to move her hand on him, pressing it down further and further, until he was pressing it against his crotch. Caterina moved up until she was close to his head and then raised herself, her hand still on him. Joe turned his head, eyes shut, and pushed his face into her breasts. He could feel them beneath the thin silk of her dress and he opened his mouth and tried to cover one of them with his lips. She moved, pressing her body against him, and slowly began to rub the hard erection she felt beneath her hand.

She continued to rub, up and down, slowly but insistently. It was only several moments before she felt him shudder. He sighed with sudden release, and as he came in his pants he murmured, 'God . . .' and his head fell back away from her breast. His eyes never opened.

How long they remained that way, Caterina wasn't sure. After some time she heard his breathing grow heavy and regular and knew he was asleep. Then and only then did she have the courage to raise herself enough to be able to look at him. He was truly asleep, his expression childlike, innocent. She freed herself with care and looked around. The food on the dining room table looked as if it'd been there for ever.

She got to her feet and went over and got a light blanket with which she covered him. Then she started to clear the table, trying to restore some semblance of normality. As she carried things out to the kitchen and returned to the kitchen, to where Joe lay sleeping, she felt as if nothing would ever be normal again. She threw brief looks at him. He was spread out, limbs and features relaxed in something approximating abandon, and the pose frightened and upset her. Finally, though everything hadn't been cleared, she sat down on a chair. Beyond the walls she could feel the silence of the city. It seemed to penetrate into the room where she sat near her sleeping son, and as she sat there, she felt as if she was being engulfed by that silence.

When Joe opened his eyes it was morning and he was alone. He was stretched out on the divan and a plaid rug had been thrown over him. He looked around and then got to his feet. He heard Concetta singing to herself as she cleaned up. He turned and saw someone sitting in the garden, reading a paper. He opened the curtains and for a moment thought it was Caterina. It was Marina. She lowered the paper and looked at him. 'Hi,' he said.

'Hi,' she said, and smiled.

'Do you have a key to our house?' he asked.

'Sit down,' she said, and began to arrange a place for him at the small table. 'I've prepared a delicious breakfast for you.'

He looked at her, and then turned and went across to the doors leading to his mother's room. He went in. The room was empty. The bed hadn't been slept in. He went back out and joined Marina at the table.

When he was sitting down she poured him some coffee. She could see he was waiting for something to be said, and after a moment she knew she wouldn't play the game any longer. 'She's gone,' she said.

Joe nodded. 'I know.'

'If you really want to know, I will tell you where she's gone.'

'Where?' Joe said, and picked up the coffee cup.

NINE

Joe caught a train mid morning. Marina had told him his mother had gone to Parma, to see her old voice teacher, but Joe couldn't understand why. All he knew was that she had abandoned him. He was going after her because he wanted to know the real reason. Voice teacher, he thought to himself with uncertain anger. Why should she go see some voice teacher?

In fact, Caterina hadn't seen her teacher. She'd first wandered across the square in front of Parma's cathedral, with the octagonal baptistry to one side. The white hot light made the stones of the eleventh-century cathedral look even more bleached with age than they were. She looked this way and that, as if something would reveal itself to her, some familiar piece of time she'd once possessed.

Her chauffeur, whom she'd roused in the middle of the night to drive her all this way, followed obediently as she made her slow tour of the small city. When she had gone to see The Pilotta, a large unfinished seventeenth-century structure built by dukes of the Farnese family, he had stayed close in case she decided she wanted to be driven, rather than walk. He had even suggested she might like to ride, but she'd refused, saying she wanted to walk.

Now she stood in the city's main square, Piazza Garibaldi. She stared for a moment at the long, low building at the north end of the piazza, the Governor's Palace, with its clock and bell tower, and three separate sundials. She looked around, and remembered the way the piazza looked in winter, fresh snow shovelled into neat little piles, like checkers. Among the piled snow, the men of Parma stood in groups of three or four, umbrellas up to shield them from the weather. Most wore the woollen Parma capes and shapeless fedora hats. They stood and discussed business and politics and sometimes it rained and sometimes it snowed and they stood there and calmly considered various subjects.

It was the Parma she remembered best. Not the baptistry, or the cathedral, but this square. She'd visited the Charterhouse once, going to stare at it because she felt somehow obliged. Stendhal had immortalized the place and she though it would be proper for her to visit it. It had bored her, she'd gained nothing from it. No, what she remembered was the wonderful old men with their beautiful faces, weathered and quick to smile. When she saw the ice-cream cart, her heart leapt with joy and she hurried over and ordered two cones. She watched the man scoop out the ice cream into the cones and when he handed them over and said, '*Prego*,' she paid him, took the cones, but instead of thanking him asked, in Italian, 'Where's Otello?'

'Not around any more,' the ice-cream vendor answered.

Caterina got back to the car and handed the driver one of the cones, saying in Italian, 'It's the best in Parma.'

'*Grazie*,' the man said, accepting the cone. He opened the door for her with his other hand, but she shook her head.

'I still want to walk,' she told him in Italian. 'Drive along behind.'

The driver nodded and got in as she set off. A moment later, the car was slowly following her as she walked along the pavement. She stared at the oncoming pedestrians as if looking for something in their faces, but there was nothing to be found. She continued like this for another hundred feet and then finally stopped and waited. The car caught up to her and the driver leaned back and opened the door for her. Caterina got in and they drove off.

As they drove along, Caterina continued to stare out at the passing people and buildings. She felt a weight in her heart, a deep sadness as well as a sense of loss. 'Nobody recognizes me in this city,' she said in Italian. They drove on and she leaned forward to gaze at a small doorway. As they passed it she turned and watched it and then said, 'I lived here.'

'Excuse me,' the driver said in Italian, 'but I thought that madame was from America.'

'I am,' she answered in Italian, adding, 'I was born in New York.'

When they came to the outskirts of Parma, the car speeded up. They drove along country roads, taking several turnings, and then as they came over the brow of a small hill Caterina leaned forward and gestured towards a one-storey house in the distance. The car slowed and then pulled over and stopped on the edge of the road. The driver got out and opened the back door. Caterina got out, her eyes on the house, her look apprehensive. 'I wonder if his sister is still alive?' she asked herself aloud.

As if on signal, an elderly woman came out of the house and stood on the threshold. She was old, stolid-looking, like a withered watchdog. Caterina walked down the road and turned in at the gate and started up the walk. The old woman stared at her closely, and then smiled as recognition flooded her face. She embraced Caterina, and then led her into the house. 'He won't know you,' she warned sadly.

Caterina nodded, and went along the hall by herself, moving as if in memory, the layout fresh in her heart. She walked confidently until she reached a closed door and hesitated. Her heart was beating wildly. She opened the door and went in.

She stood on the threshold of the room, a room full of large windows. A man sat huddled in a wheelchair. Music scores were piled up wherever the eye looked. And there were photographs, scenic sketches, and phonograph records. Caterina stared at the man, who returned her gaze.

'Maestro,' she exclaimed softly, uncertain if he even saw her. She took a step closer, wanting to rush over and embrace him. A ray of sunlight shone into the room and the old man turned and gripped the wheels and slowly moved his chair into the warm beams. She stepped in front of him, causing him to look up at her again. 'I've come a long way to see you.' She wasn't sure he'd actually heard her. 'I'm sorry I stopped writing to you.' She bent to peer at him carefully. 'You don't even know who I am, do you?' she asked, but she wasn't certain.

She straightened and forced herself to look at the musty disorder of years. ‘Oh, God,’ she sighed, her voice shaking, ‘I spent so much time in this room.’ She moved along the wall full of records, and suddenly had to catch herself on the arm of a chair. ‘Oh, I feel faint . . .’ She made herself sit down and took a deep breath to clear her head.

After several she looked over at him. He seemed to be watching her without expression. ‘Breathing exercise.’ She gave a wan smile. ‘You were a tyrant. I didn’t believe in myself. You taught me how to take care of my voice, how to use my voice, that it was beautiful, that I could sell it.’ She took another deep breath and forced herself to stand. She made sure she felt steady, and then continued her slow tour, constantly turning her head to address herself directly to him. ‘That I was strong,’ she continued. ‘That’s all that mattered to us, my voice. I wanted to be always singing, singing. That’s all that mattered.’ She saw him reach for the wheels once more as the rays of sun shifted imperceptibly but steadily. ‘You’re vain, you are.’ She went closer to him. ‘Selfish.’ A small sense of relief touched her heart and she came even closer. ‘How come I never talked to you before?’ She watched him move himself into the sun’s warmth once again. ‘Are you looking for the spotlight?’

She turned, and went over to a dusty old cloth over the piano. She touched it and looked back at him, realizing the cover had been there for a long long time. ‘The piano’s been covered.’ She looked around again and realized the piano stool was the only thing she could sit on.

She picked it up and carried it and placed it by the wheelchair and sat down. ‘Do you remember when you told me, “One day you’ll hate your voice?”’ She took another deep breath, but not because she felt dizzy. She was afraid, more so than ever, and it had come over her in the last moments, as she spoke. ‘That’s why I came here,’ she forced herself to say. ‘I don’t want to sing any more. I have rehearsals for *Ballo*, and I don’t want to go.’ She leaned closer to him. ‘I’m like you. I’m finished.’ She half rose to peer at him at close range. ‘Can you hear me?’ she asked with a note of desperation. ‘I’m finished! Don’t you even hear me?’

She couldn't tell where the ancient man, her maestro, so cherished, so feared, was gazing. And when she heard the falsetto voice start to sing she thought, for a moment, it was coming out of the very air. And then she realized it was he. '*Soave sia il vento,*' he began softly, the voice thin, his lips stretching with the effort. He stopped and reached over to an ancient tape recorder and pushed one of the buttons. The music began, the music for this trio from Mozart's *Cosi Fan Tutte.*

Caterina leaned closer to him, and sang with the three singers on the tape, her eyes on her teacher's lips as they pronounced the sweet words: '*gently blows the wind, the waves are tranquil, the elements are all kind to our desire* . . .' It was a moment in that opera when lovers have taken their leave on what seems a perilous journey, and those left behind invoke their safety with cautious words of loving reason. As Caterina sang and the music rose lightly into the air of the small room, she reached out and rested her hand on her teacher's shoulder with the most infinite tenderness. Whatever she had come to ask him, whatever she thought he might tell her, it seemed to her now that the words they sang were the answer he wanted to give her.

The music ended, and she gazed down at him and said, 'I used to sing that to my son when he was a little boy.' She went over and looked out of the window. A taxi slowed and stopped in front of the house. It took her a moment to realize that the person getting out of it was Joe.

She came running out of the house and hurried down the walk. 'Joe!' she cried. 'I'm so glad to see you. How did you find me here?'

'Marina told me,' he said, eyeing her with uncertainty, wondering why she was so glad to see him.

'Thank you for coming,' she said. 'Oh,' she sighed and put her arms around him, 'I missed you.'

The chauffeur opened the door for them and Joe got in, followed by Caterina, who slowed to throw one last glance back at the house.

They were on the road back to Parma when Joe turned to her and said, 'Why did you leave?'

Caterina reacted as if she'd been expecting the question. Her answer came quickly, and sounded half apologetic. 'I had to. I needed to be back here. And I—' she faltered, '—to see my teacher. I just wanted to be here.' She had wanted to be more positive, more emphatic. She turned and stared out of the window at the countryside passing by, and for a moment wondered to herself, why did I come here?

'Oh, bullshit!' Joe exclaimed, snapping her out of her brief reverie. 'You took off for the hell of it and you know it.' He was hurt, and angry at her, and she'd abandoned him just when he believed something special had happened.

Caterina turned to him, and didn't have it in her to get angry with him. 'Joe,' she began, 'would you stop?' There was a beseeching smile on her face as she went on. 'I'm very weak.' She half closed her eyes, covered them with one hand, and sank deeper into the car's seat. 'I'm exhausted. You're killing me. I'm dying.'

'No you're not,' Joe said with sarcasm. 'You're immortal.' She opened her eyes and stared at him. 'I've seen you die lots of times on stage,' he went on, 'and I stopped believing you.' For some reason this pleased her and she smiled. 'You were fake then,' he added, 'and you're still a fake.' The smile faded and she stared at him for another moment and then turned and resumed looking out of the window.

They were rolling along one of Parma's broad avenues when she suddenly sat forward and her expression changed. '*Ferma!*' she ordered the driver, '*ferma qui.*' The car stopped as she'd ordered and she jumped out.

Joe followed her and they found themselves standing in front of a grand columned building. A sign on one of the porticos said: Teatro Regio. It was Parma's Opera House. Caterina stared at it, and began to talk, a flow of words. 'We opened the season here with *Traviata.* It was December 26th, and it was snowing outside. It snowed for two days. God . . .' she gave a small helpless gesture and turned to Joe and went on. 'I was in my hotel room, throwing up. I threw up on everything. I came here, and I threw up on my costume. It was a white dress, and

I had to wear it inside out. My God, I was so nervous! It was my first Violetta. And then, at the end of the performance, it was incredible.' She clasped herself and spun slowly around, as if the memory was making her move, dizzying her. 'The audience, they were, they were wild. Wild. I was drunk with applause.' She slowed, and turned back to consider her son, standing listening to her. 'I didn't want anything else but that.' Her hands slowly lowered to her sides, and she smiled. 'And then I found out I was pregnant.' She cocked her head, and looked from her son up at the façade of the theatre before them. 'Your father fainted.'

Joe had listened, partly fascinated, partly annoyed. But when she told him about his father he'd pricked up his ears, and took a step closer to her. 'Will you ever get married again?' She didn't seem to be listening to him. She'd taken a step and then another towards the theatre, and was staring at the front door. 'Will you?' he repeated.

'This theatre is closed,' she said with quiet disgust and turned away.

Joe followed her back to where the car stood. The driver hopped out again obediently and swung the back door open for them.

Caterina started to get in, and then stopped and looked at the driver. 'Leave us,' she said in Italian. 'I want to drive.' She opened the driver's door and got into his place. 'We'll see you back here in a few hours.' She waved for Joe, and he came around and got in next to her. She started the car and rolled down the window, and gave the driver a wave.

'Okay,' he said and watched the car drive off.

'Where're we going now?' Joe demanded, and turned to look out of the window. He found the whole place boring.

'I want to show you something,' she answered. 'I want you to see a bit of this countryside.'

'What's so special about it?' he said.

They drove back out of town, crossed a small bridge, and then drove under a colonnade of arched trees. Joe sat staring glumly out of the window. She slowed down as the car neared a crossroads. 'That's where he kissed me,' she said, her voice distant. Joe glanced over at her and then looked at an ornate little villa with a fountain in front of it.

'Who?'

'Your father,' she said, and stopped the car.

'Where?'

'Here,' she said, indicating the villa and the crossroads.

'Here where?' he demanded. 'Here?' He pointed. 'Here?' He pointed in another direction. 'In the grass? Must be here. Maybe in there. Tell me where! Where?'

Caterina looked at him calmly. 'Here.' She stared at him for a moment, and then leaned over and kissed him on the lips. She moved back, their eyes gazing at one another, and then Joe moved forward and kissed her. It was a small kiss, but it was direct, and she looked at him for but a moment before she leaned back to him and kissed him, long and hard, on the mouth. He returned the kiss, moving his head to open her mouth under his. The kiss became more passionate, longer, wetter, and it was finally with a small gasp that they separated. She stared at him, her eyes bright, and then turned her attention back to the road and started up the car.

They had driven along some time, neither saying anything, when she said, 'I bet I can find it,' Joe turned to ask her something but she simply added, 'the house that we lived in. Oh,' she went on with unexpected enthusiasm, 'I want to show it to you, Joe. It was so sweet. It was little and it had a grape arbour behind it. It had a little vegetable garden that we took care of. It had two enormous walnut trees, and poplars all around. We lived there for, oh almost a year, I think, and then we moved to the sea, close to Rome.' As she spoke, she was staring out at the passing scene, slowing to catch the names of roads they were passing. 'I think this is the way.'

Joe watched her looking at the markers, and finally said, 'Are we lost?'

'Not at all,' she said confidently, and drove on.

'Ah!' she exclaimed so suddenly that Joe jumped. He sat forward and peered through the windshield. 'What is it?' he said, 'do you see the house?' There was a farm on one side, across a field, with a road turning into it some fifty yards ahead of them.

'Yes,' she said decisively. 'I know where we are.'

When she drove past the turn-off, he turned to her. 'Where?'

'That farm over there,' she said and nodded in another direction. Joe looked and saw the buildings she meant. 'Do you see that farm? That's where we used to get the fresh bread.'

'Oh, Mom,' Joe pleaded, 'I'm hungry. Please, I haven't eaten since last night.'

'I know where we are,' Caterina said with complete confidence.

They turned down the small dirt road leading to the farm, drove into the yard, and stopped. They got out and while Caterina walked around in front, staring at the buildings, assessing them, somehow reluctant to get too close, Joe went around in back. When he returned, she was where he'd left her, walking back and forth in front of the place as if looking at some sort of a piece of art. 'Amazing,' she said with great sincerity.

She had the same expression on her face when they were back in the car, driving along down the road. 'That is amazing to me, that farm. It's as if the world stopped. It's exactly the way it was when I was there before. The same people. It's incredible.' She gave a small shake of her head and the wonderment stayed in her look.

'They make fresh bread back there,' Joe said.

'I know,' Caterina said, and drove on. 'Now I really want to show you the house we lived in,' she repeated.

Joe was looking out of the windows, craning his neck to catch sight of distant houses set beyond hedges and clumps of trees. 'It's got to be around here.'

It wasn't. They drove on, and Caterina had a look of disappointment as she continued to slow at intersections to examine road signs. 'We've been driving around for hours,' Joe said to her.

'I know,' she admitted, and again brightened unexpectedly. 'Ah, ah! That! It's the next turn here on the right.'

They took the turn, but there was nothing, just another road lined with the same trees and hedges.

'We're lost,' Joe said disdainfully.

Caterina's hands were tighter on the wheel as she stared at the road ahead of them. 'Maybe to the left,' she said, with little confidence. She took the left, but once more the road looked no different, and there were no houses visible. 'My teacher was the most important, the most famous—' she slowed, eyes searching, and then added, 'the most famous maestro around here.'

Joe listened with little interest and turned to her with a sarcastic expression on his face. 'And he fell in love with you.'

She threw him a glance and said, 'He fell in love with my voice.' A road approached and she squinted, trying to read its name. 'Shit . . .' she said softly to herself under her breath.

'Ma, hey, let's eat,' Joe said. 'Okay?'

Caterina had no idea where they were. But what she'd said about the maestro opened up new memories, things she'd seen when she'd walked into that musty room and seen the old man in his wheelchair. She'd heard things, forgotten things, and had found herself remembering herself in a way she felt was important, very important. 'Do you know that I worked solidly for two years, I didn't do anything else. My voice was the most important thing in the world to me. Do you know what he would have me do? He would have me lie down on the ground and he would make me sing and he would stand on my diaphragm, to strengthened it, because I had a weak voice.' She stopped for a moment. 'He wanted me to be the greatest singer in the world.'

If Joe could have sounded and looked more bored, more put out, he would have. 'Are you telling me the story of your life?' he drawled.

'Yes,' Caterina said candidly.

Joe began to hum and then broke into the MacDonald's song: '*Two all-beef patties, special sauce, lettuce, cheese, pickles, onions on a sloppy old bun.*'

Caterina smiled and looked over at him. 'You have a great voice, Joe.'

Joe sneered, and looked out of the window. Then his expression changed to open annoyance. 'Ma,' he said, 'this is the third time we've passed this church.'

'I know, I know,' Caterina said nodding. 'I know.' She slowed down, and then stopped. 'I can't find the house. I give up.'

'I'm starving,' Joe said accusingly.

'I know,' Caterina said wanly. 'I know.'

Joe dug around in his pocket and came up empty-handed. 'I don't have any more gum.'

Caterina nodded. 'I know.' She shook her head. 'I don't know what to do,' she said and began to hum.

'*Keep on rockin' me, baby,*' Joe started to sing.

Caterina gave him a pained look. 'God, if you become a rock n' roll singer, I'll kill myself.' She pressed down on the accelerator and the car started off once more.

'*Keep on rockin'*,' Joe sang plaintively.

The car hit a bump and lurched. Caterina fought the wheel and made a face. 'This car isn't made for country roads.' She pulled over and stopped again. She took a deep breath, and rolled down the window and looked out. 'Oh, God,' she exclaimed, 'look at the crops. Look at the crops, Joe.' She saw something and pointed. 'This might be the house over here.'

Joe leaned to get a look. 'It is?'

Caterina stared, and then gave a small shake of her head. 'I mean, no, it's just a farm.' She was looking for something to make her feel enthusiastic. 'Look at the grapes.' It wasn't working. 'Look at the cows.'

'Shitting all over the place,' Joe said at her elbow.

She didn't give him the satisfaction of a look and instead pointed to a rise where willows grew. 'Look at that. Isn't that beautiful?' She started up again. 'That landscape?' She picked up speed and came to yet another road. 'I think this is the road.' The car turned, and headed down it. 'Oh, look at that.' She was looking for small pleasures in anything. 'Oh, that ancient tractor.' A house appeared from behind some trees and she slowed. 'Joe,' she said more quietly, 'maybe this is the house.'

He stared at it and then looked at her. 'Is it?'

She let the car roll past it without slowing to a stop. 'No,' she said after a long moment.

They continued along the road. Joe was moving restlessly, uncomfortable in the seat. 'Are you sure this is the road?' Caterina said nothing. They came to another farm, with a large vegetable garden. 'Tomatoes,' he said.

'Corn,' she said looking at the stalks passing by, 'bigger than you are.' And with sudden excitement she added, 'Here we go, here we go!'

'The house?' Joe asked, suspicious of her now. She said nothing, and he gave her a knowing look.

'Joe,' she said, 'what kind of trees are those?'

He turned as she pointed. 'I don't know,' he said. It was truly a strange cluster of twisted trunks and spreading branches. 'They're really weird.'

Caterina rolled down the window and took a deep breath. 'God, smell this earth.'

'Yes,' Joe said with a sharp laugh. 'Smell this shit.'

The road curved and when they came around it Caterina saw some houses nearby. 'There's four houses over there,' she said. 'I don't remember four houses.'

'Maybe they built another one,' Joe suggested.

'Right,' she agreed. 'There was a corn field, and there are the grape vines.' They came closer, and she shook her head with disappointment. 'No, it was closer to the road.'

The road was getting rougher and as they drove on Caterina had to steer to keep the car out of the ruts. 'I don't think these city cars were made for these roads.' They came around a corner, and there was a paved road and a crossroads. Caterina came to a sudden stop that made Joe lurch forward.

He caught himself on the dashboard and glared at his mother. 'What're you doing, for Christ's sake!'

'Look,' she said, staring. A large, peaceful-looking house sat in the midst of tall, stately trees. The house itself was squarish, ochre-yellow in colour, with freshly painted green shutters on all of the windows. It was a villa, a small villa with a lovely garden around it. The entrance was across the paved road, and as Joe looked across at the house he noticed a sign on the highway, with an arrow pointing in one direction. The sign said BUSSETO. 'Look what I found!' Caterina said with genuine delight and amazement. 'Look where we are, Joe. This is Verdi's house. We're in Sant'Agata.'

'Yeah?' Joe said, unimpressed.

'Joe,' Caterina said, unwilling to let her enthusiasm be dampened in any way, 'this is where he wrote all his operas, this was his world. The land, this house, they were his inspiration, his vision. He'd look out of the window, see an old hunchbacked peasant, and it would become *Rigoletto*.'

'So what?' Joe said.

'Everything came from this place,' Caterina insisted more heatedly. 'He'd see the Po River, but he would think of the Nile, Egypt, Spain. *Aida*, Joe.' She made to open her door as she turned to him. 'Come on, do you want to see it?'

'Not particularly,' Joe said.

'Not particularly,' Caterina repeated with a nod. She reclosed her door and sat for a moment, staring across at the charming villa and its suggestion of another world, another time. 'I don't understand you,' she said.

She started the car and turned on to the paved road. The villa passed them. Her eyes stayed on it. 'This is my family,' she explained, resentment slowly rising inside her, 'it's like me, it's like my father. Verdi.' The villa was past them. She turned down another unpaved road and picked up speed.

After several moments, she turned and stared hard at her son. 'Jesus, don't you care about anything. You're lost.' Her eyes flicked back to the road. 'You're a fucking junkie!' She said it quietly, but the tightness in her voice was like a sharp little crackle. Whether she knew what she was doing or not, her foot slowly pressed down on the accelerator. The car picked up speed instantly. Soon, the trees were whipping past. 'Just a junkie,' she declared in an empty voice. 'That's all.'

The speedometer continued to climb, until Joe saw it passing 120 kilometres an hour, over eighty-five miles an hour. The car roared down the road, dust spiralling up behind it. Joe's eyes went to her face and stared at her. Her expression was set, her jaw rigid, her hands gripping the wheel impassively. He felt the car give another little jump and looked back at the speedometer and they were going almost 140 kilometres an hour. 'Oh, my God,' he cried as they careened around a corner. He grabbed the dashboard to keep his balance and stared out. They were hurtling down the road, trees and hedges a blinding blur. Suddenly, there was a muffled *crack* and the car veered sharply, almost ran off into a ditch, and then weaved dangerously as it slowed down. Caterina's knuckles were white on the wheel, and her eyes didn't move from the road. Her foot was off the accelerator, and it was some distance before they came finally to an unsteady stop, rocking the last several yards.

Joe was out and running across the road as if expecting the car to explode, screaming, 'Are you nuts? What are you trying to do, kill me?' He was waving his arms, almost hopping with angry fear. 'Are you fucking crazy?'

Caterina sat for a moment without looking at him. Then she said, 'Relax, it's nothing serious.' She got out of the car and went around and saw the flattened tyre. Joe was right behind her. 'See, it's a flat tyre.' She went back to get the ignition key and then returned and opened the trunk. She began to take out the things she would need to change the tyre. 'It'll just take a second.'

'Mom,' he said, 'do you want me to help you?'

'No,' she said, too angry at the moment to want him around. She got the jack under the rear fender and began to crank the car up. 'Go listen to the radio,' she told him and tossed him the keys. But he stayed where he was, watching her. 'Stop staring over my shoulder, it makes me nervous. Go on,' she waved. He went back and got into the car. Caterina resumed jacking it up.

It took her almost ten minutes to change the tyre, but finally it was done and she let the car slowly come back down to rest on the ground. She hauled out the jack and tossed it back into the trunk, along with the blown tyre. She was covered with oil and grime, her skirt smeared and her face smudged. She was less angry than she had been but tired from the exertion – along with the long, futile search she'd been making – and slammed down the trunk lid. 'So!' she announced, and headed for the driver's side where she could hear Joe listening to some noisy music on the car radio.

Suddenly, the engine came to life and the car started to move. She stared at it and watched it come to a stop about thirty feet away. She set off after it, the anger back in her face. 'Sometimes,' she cried, 'being your mother can be a real pain in the ass!' The car suddenly moved off again, only this time it didn't slow down but picked up speed. 'You stop, you little shit!' she cried after it. 'Come back here.' A moment later, it rounded a curve and was gone. 'Fuck!' Caterina exclaimed with disgust and actually kicked at the dirt.

She looked around and realized she was in the middle of nowhere. There was a kilometre marker nearby and she went over to it and sat down. She thought Joe might turn around and come back for her, but she knew him better than that. He was pissed off, trying to get even with her over something. He wasn't coming back. She got up, and started to walk.

She walked for quite some time and her feet hurt when she came to another kilometre marker and sat down on it. Then, far down the road, she heard a car coming. She scowled, thinking to herself, so the little prick is coming back for me. She looked up just in time to see it wasn't her car but another one. She jumped to her feet and held out her hand, partly to wave for the driver to stop, partly a kind of hitchhiking gesture.

The car slowed and then stopped. She hurried over to it as the driver, a heavy-set man in his late forties leaned over from the driver's side and opened the door. 'Problems?' he asked in Italian.

'Could you give me a lift?' she asked him.

'Sure,' the man said and gestured for her to get into the car. Caterina climbed in and closed the door behind her. 'Where's your car?' he asked in Italian, picking up speed. 'Don't tell me it's been stolen.'

'No,' she said with a shake of her head. She eased herself into the soft cushions of the seat, and felt the strain in her feet and legs. After a moment she looked over at the man to study him a bit. He was florid-faced, obviously well fed, and he wore a well-cut suit, a fine shirt, a handsome tie with a gold pin.

The man looked over and grinned, showing lots of teeth. 'American?'

Caterina nodded. 'Yes.'

He reached above to the visor and pulled several paper tissues out of a concealed holder. He held them out for her to take. She nodded again, and turned his rear-view mirror so she could see where the dirt was on her face. He lowered her visor and showed her that he had put a mirror there especially for the convenience of his passengers, and returned the rear-view mirror to its proper position.

Caterina nodded her thanks yet again, and began to clean up her dirtied face. It was some moments before she realized the man was holding something for her to see. It was a photograph. She took it and saw two men, on what looked like the back of a fishing boat. One of the two men was in Army fatigues, had a beard, and was leaning back, looking expansive. 'Castro,' the man was saying to her.

Caterina looked at the picture and said, 'I wish I had his boots.'

'*Si*,' the man answered, not sure what she'd said, and put away the photograph.

They drove along a while, the man handling the wheel casually, letting her see he enjoyed manoeuvring his fine car along these picturesque lanes. He turned to her with a broad grin and said, 'Now I want tell you something that will shock you—'

Oh, Christ, Caterina thought to herself as she took in the look on his face.

'—as American.'

Caterina waited a second, trying not to look too expectant.

Without much of a pause, the man said, 'I am a Communist.' That seemed to satisfy him enormously and he adjusted his broad shoulders and returned his attention to the road.

Caterina gazed at him quizzically and then said, 'So?'

The man turned back to her. 'I am a Communist,' he explained and with a tilt of his head indicated her. 'You are American.'

Looking bemused, Caterina stared a moment, and then said, 'Stop the car. *Fermi.*'

Upset, the man slowed, turning from her to the road, back and forth, not knowing exactly what had happened. 'I've offended you,' he said apologetically. 'Forgive me.'

Caterina pointed and the man turned and saw the small *hostaria* nearby. 'I'm not offended,' she said. 'I'm hungry. Will you join me?'

The man pulled in and parked next to another car already parked there. He got out and closed his door as Caterina got out her side and came around to join him. They walked along the small paved path leading to the inn's front door. Caterina paid no attention to the other car. It was hers.

TEN

Joe had been at the inn for almost half an hour. When his mother and the man she was with came in, he had a table full of food in front of him and the innkeeper was holding yet another tray. 'Look,' he was saying proudly, showing Joe the sliced culatello on the plate. Joe sat at a small table near a window out of which the rose-streaked sky of sunset was visible. 'You don't understand me,' the innkeeper was saying in Italian, 'but I don't understand your language either. I'll tell you about this just the same.'

Caterina and the Communist took a table near Joe's and the Communist turned and signalled to the innkeeper. 'A bottle of Savignon – ' the Communist called over 'and two . . .'

The innkeeper meanwhile had another tray to show Joe, a different cured meat, and was saying, always in Italian, 'This salt-meat is made only here. It has to cure in fog, in still air, and after two years you get . . .' and without continuing he took a small piece and passed it to Joe, who sniffed it, closed his eyes as if in ecstasy, and sighed loudly, 'Ahhhhh.'

The innkeeper was delighted with Joe's reaction and said, 'It's as sweet as if it had been made just now. That is our secret.'

Once Joe was eating merrily, the innkeeper brought wine and hams to Caterina and her companion. She pointedly wouldn't look at Joe, who was eating energetically, slurping his wine with gusto and following it with ravenous bites of bread and salami. She smiled at the Communist as he poured her wine, and when he made a small grimace, she laughed, lightly and trillingly.

Joe studied the two of them. The man with his mother was jovial, and big. He was leaning over to make a point with her, pushing his chair back to laugh as he poured her more wine and then tore off pieces of the rough country bread for both of them. He got up and began telling a story.

'Six years ago in Cuba,' he was telling Caterina, 'fishing.'

'Cuba,' Caterina said.

The man took out the photograph and poked a finger at one of the figures. 'Fidel.'

The innkeeper reappeared with another tray to show Joe. 'This is this year's,' he said in Italian.

'Fidel,' the Communist repeated, and put away the photograph.

'*Si*, Fidel,' Caterina echoed.

'Castro,' the man said, nodded to the picture, and looked to see if she realized what he was telling her. 'Same boat. Two men: Fidel, and me.' He waited for her to understand. 'Fishing,' he explained further, and put down the picture so that he could spread both hands far apart as he said, 'I fished *cosi grande* – this big. Fidel—' his hands came together and almost met in a clap 'very little. Very jealous.' He looked solemnly at her and then burst into thunderous laughter.

'Fidel, *bello*,' the man was saying, 'beautiful man. *Forte*. But,' he raised a finger in warning, 'very jealous for my big fish.'

'Jealous,' Caterina agreed and laughed. 'I bet.' She picked up her wine and clinked glasses with him. '*Cin, cin*.'

'What an asshole!' Joe muttered loud enough for the others to hear.

The man with his mother paused and half turned in his chair to look over to where Joe sat. 'He want something with us?' he asked in Italian, turning back to her.

'No,' she said. 'A punk.' For a brief moment her eyes went to Joe and met his. Then she tore off a small piece of ham and fed it to the Communist. 'A little punk,' she enunciated slowly. She watched the man chew the ham, and then reached over and felt his arm. 'You're strong,' she said with a warm smile. 'Do you do a lot of sports?'

The man gestured, a toss of his hand over his shoulder. 'A long time ago.'

'And now?'

The innkeeper came up to Joe carrying a bottle of wine which was held aloft, like some sort of a trophy. 'Listen,' he said in Italian, 'I want you to taste this wine here. It's a Trebbiano.'

Caterina took some bread and tore it apart and then put some ham on it. 'A piccolo sandwich for a big man,' she said to the Communist, and fed it to him. He ate it in one gulp as she made another. He took it from her and put it on his open palm.

'*Guardi*,' he said – 'watch,' and slapped his wrist so that the food popped straight into his mouth.

Caterina guffawed, and said, 'Let me try that.'

The innkeeper poured out two glasses for Joe, taking one for himself, tasting it, and then saying to Joe, 'You like it?'

Joe tasted it and then smacked his lips and declared, '*Bellissimo!*' He toasted his host, and emptied the glass with a flourish.

'*Grazie, grazie*,' the innkeeper said, pleased.

'No, no,' the Communist was saying to Caterina as she didn't get the food into her mouth. 'Like so,' and he repeated the little flip.

'Again,' she urged him.

He did it again and she tried it and he said, 'Very good. One, two, three – hup!' but she did it wrong and he shook his head. 'No.' He saw that her face was still dirty, and reached over to wipe her cheek.

'*Sporca?*' she asked him. 'Is it dirty?'

He continued to wipe gently, staring into her eyes, and asked, '*Sposata?* Married?'

Before she could answer, they were interrupted by Joe, who began to drum on the table and plates with his knife and fork. He beat a steady rhythm, developing a hard-driving tattoo that built and built, until it became a true solo, full of virtuoso effects, the knife and fork whirring out to hit glasses and smaller plates as all the time he maintained a rattling beat on the table itself. He finished with a terrific flourish, and collapsed back into his chair.

'Bravo!' the innkeeper said and burst into applause. 'Really good. He didn't break a single glass.' He brought out another bottle of wine. 'This is Malvasia, three years old, straight.' He poured Joe a glass, and then brought the wine over and poured two glasses for Caterina and the Communist.

When they had drunk it, the Communist signalled for the bill.

'Three thousand,' the innkeeper said, bringing it over.

The man dropped several notes on the plate, added a generous tip, and said, '*Grazie.*'

Joe watched them get up from their table and go out into the small glass-enclosed foyer. He saw Caterina catch the man by the arm and saw something to him. The man turned, his expression questioning. Caterina nodded, and squeezed the man's arm. He nodded, and went out of the door to the parking lot. Caterina turned, and came back into the restaurant.

'Do you have a room?' she asked the innkeeper in Italian. Joe understood the word '*camera*' for *room* and saw the innkeeper nod and point to the back of the establishment.

'Sure, definitely,' he was saying in Italian, and began to sing, in deep throbbing voice, the gypsy woman's aria from the second act of *Il Trovatore*: '*She was in chains as she was led to her terrible fate, her babe in her arms. I followed, weeping—*'

Joe couldn't believe what was happening. He rose, and turned to stare after his mother as she went off, and then he heard the sound of a car engine come to life in the parking lot and moments later drive away. He turned back, and hurried after his mother and the innkeeper.

He led Caterina to a small bedroom at the back of the inn, still singing the terrible aria: '. . . *in vain did the wretched woman try to stop and bless me* . . .' Caterina disappeared into the room, and with a courtly low bow the innkeeper took his leave of her as Joe came up behind him. He cast a baleful eye at Joe, singing, '. . . *and in a broken voice, she cried, "Avenge me."* '

Caterina stood in the middle of the room, waiting for Joe to come in. He saw her, and slowed. 'How could you let him touch you?' he said. 'He was such a jerk. And you touched him, too.'

'I didn't want to,' she said ,and came over to him. 'I wanted to be touching you. You're right, he was an asshole, he was a jerk, he was awful.'

She took his face in her hands and began to kiss him, and then led him to the bed. He sat down on the edge and she sat next to him. She could feel him trembling. 'I'm scared, too,' she whispered, and began to take off his shirt. 'I'm scared, too.' She got his shirt off and began to run her hands over his back. 'Oh, oh, God,' she murmured, 'your back is so soft. Beautiful.' She began to kiss it. 'Oh, baby, my baby, my baby.' She slowly turned him to gaze into his large soft eyes. 'Let's not fight any more.'

Joe stared at her, and said, 'Your face is a mess. I'll clean it up.' And he leaned forward and began to lick her. His tongue moved up her cheek to her forehead, and then across her eyes down to her mouth, licking harder and harder.

'Good,' she said passionately. 'It feels good.'

He gripped her head with both hands. 'No,' he said when he thought she was moving away from him, 'not finished. Hold still.'

'Joe,' she moaned, 'Joe.' Her passion flared uncontrollably. 'Joe, Joe.' She spread her legs, reached down and with one hand dragged her dress up above her knees, to her waist. She was wearing small blue bikini panties, and for a moment she couldn't stop herself and began to rub herself, moving beneath her own touch. Her eyes closed and she fell back on the bed, writhing. Then she pulled his head down with her other hand, and pressed it on to herself.

Joe could feel the hard pubic bone under his cheek. 'Mom,' he said, and a sudden helplessness and fear overtook him. 'Mom.' He was unable to move because she continued to press him down into herself.

'Joe,' she moaned. 'Oh, God, I love you, Joe. I love you. I love you.'

'No,' he said, and slowly pulled away from her, 'you don't. You hate me. You've never loved me.' His anger grew, exploding slowly through him as he stared down at her, eyes opening slowly, the glisten of passion still in them. 'You've always hated me. Always. You're crazy! You're crazy!'

He grabbed her by the hair and shook her violently. 'Fucking liar!' he cried, and Caterina for the first time thought he was going to kill her. 'You hate me, you hate me, goddammit!' He had completely lost control. His other hand went to her hair and he slammed it repeatedly into the pillow. 'Fucking bitch! You bitch! You bitch! You bitch!'

He let go suddenly, let go and stood up, and went off, into the small adjoining room. Caterina tried to catch her breath. She didn't know for a moment what had happened, and shook with fear. She swallowed air, and whimpered, helpless and terrified.

Joe was in the bathroom. He washed his face, and then slowly pulled the belt out of his pants.

He went back, ignoring Caterina who lay with her eyes closed, one hand thrown across her face, her back to him, and got his jacket and took it back to the small bathroom. His works were in one of the pockets. He got them out, arranged them on the small table, got a match, and lit the stub of candle he had brought with him.

'If only we could've found the house,' he heard Caterina say in a low, sad voice. 'It was so important to me.' He set the candle on the table, and got out a small silvery packet and carefully unwrapped it. 'I wanted you to see it,' she was saying. 'I wanted you to know.' He poured the powder into the spoon, and then added enough water to bring the level just below the edge of the spoon. 'This is very hard to say, Joe,' he heard her saying. 'I tried to tell you. I wanted to.' He held the spoon over the candle, and waited for it to bubble. His eyes flicked for a moment over to the hypo, to make sure it was near when he would be ready to fill it. 'I didn't know how,' Caterina said. The liquid was about to bubble. Joe reached for the hypo, and got ready to fill it.

Caterina slowly pushed herself up, looked around, saw the open door of the bathroom, and said, 'I thought if we could see the house where we lived,' she hesitated, swallowed, and went on, 'with your father. Not Douglas, but with your real father.'

Joe had the half-filled hypo in his hand when he heard her words. He slowed, and then put the hypo on the table. He undid the belt from around his upper arm and slipped it off. He got up, and went to stand in the open doorway. He saw her sitting up on the bed, staring at him. 'My father?' he said, and she nodded.

ELEVEN

They drove back into Rome about nine in the morning, moving slowly through the heavy traffic. Cars were bumper to bumper, inching along skittishly, the odd driver recklessly darting out to zoom ahead in the wrong lane until an oncoming car forced him to swerve dangerously back into the general flow.

Caterina had been sleeping but now she watched where they were going. Their chauffeur looked exhausted, and moved the car ahead as best he could. At times he'd lock eyes with another driver inches away, and one or the other would move their lips soundlessly, jaws working. When there was any kind of a break ahead, all the cars would spring forward, like unleashed whippets. But it was a progress of only a few feet at best, and once more everything would come to a standstill, thousands of car engines running, the cars themselves held at bay like panting beasts. There was another opening and the chauffeur made to shift into gear and get into it when an Alfa somehow appeared to twist past him and fill the space. '*Mannagia*—' the chauffeur swore under his breath and whacked the steering wheel with his gloved hand.

'Here,' Caterina said, and indicated a street which they could turn into.

The chauffeur nodded, relieved to be getting out of the general mess, and made the turn.

'Joe,' Caterina said softly, and reached down to shake him. He was asleep, his head in her lap. 'Joe.' She looked up, saw another street approaching, and said, 'Here,' to the driver.

He made another turn, and picked up speed.

'No,' she said, 'go slow.' She studied the buildings, recognized the one she was looking for, and told him, 'that one. *Fermi.* Stop.'

They pulled up in front of a school building. Caterina gazed at it and then looked back down at Joe. 'We're here,' she said gently.

Joe opened his eyes, and sat up. He looked around, half-stretching. 'What?'

'We're here,' she repeated, and pointed to the building.

A look of expectation appeared on his face, and he reached for the door handle. He opened it, and slowed only to look back at her.

'Go,' she urged him. 'Go, go.'

He jumped out of the car, and started across the pavement to the school's big iron gates.

Caterina watched him, and then leaned forward and told the driver, 'Let's keep going.'

When they got to the apartment building, she saw a figure move out from behind a corner and stand, waiting. It was Mustafa and as the car came to a stop, she heard him say, 'Joe?'

He saw her get out of the car and waited, as if thinking Joe was right behind her. 'He's not with me,' she told him.

'Where is he?' Mustafa asked.

'. . . I don't know,' Caterina lied.

Mustafa peered at her a moment, and must have taken her lie for some sort of reluctance on her part because he said, 'Is anything the matter?'

'No,' she said. 'Everything is fine.'

'Good,' he said, and flashed her his warm grin. 'Everything fine with me, too.'

'What do you want with Joe?' she said, cautious.

'Say goodbye.' He gestured. 'Mustafa leaving.'

'Oh,' she said.

'I come say goodbye to my only friend.' He gave her another big grin. 'When he come back?'

'I don't know,' she said, this time telling the truth. 'Can I tell him—' she started, and broke off.

'Tell him goodbye,' Mustafa finished for her. 'I think of him.'

*

Joe was not thinking of Mustafa. The porter had pointed out the door into the school building, saying in Italian, 'That's the door.'

Joe nodded and started for it, and then slowed. He felt his heart beating wildly. He wanted to take a deep breath, but it stuck in his throat. He got hold of the doorknob, turned it, and opened the door. He hesitated, and made himself go in.

The first thing that struck him was the light. It was a room full of light, and full of children. They were all about ten years old, and none of them had their shoes on. Joe started to look around, and heard a man's pleasant voice say, in Italian, 'All right, kids. How's it coming?'

Joe looked up, and saw his father.

The man was tall, with broad shoulders. He looked a bit heavy, but he had clear kind eyes and as he looked at the children in the classroom, a small smile seemed to be lingering on his face. He was somewhere in his forties, with a nice moustache and dark hair. He didn't seem to have noticed Joe and was paying attention to the work the children were doing.

A big piece of blue paper had been unrolled and covered almost all of the floor in the room. Joe noticed that many pairs of shoes were lined up against one of the walls. The kids were crawling all over the paper, drawing, using coloured chalks, felt pens, and spray cans. 'Like this, teacher?' one of the boys asked in Italian.

The blue paper was the sky and the kids were drawing constellations, planets, the rings of Saturn and the moon. They were creating their own special planetarium. 'That's good,' the teacher told the boy in Italian and turned to one of the other children and said, 'Bring me a pencil from over there.' He was handed the pencil and kneeled to help a girl who was drawing a series of sparkling comets. The girl had two long braids down her back and a solemn expression, and as she leaned over the blue paper, one of her braids kept falling over her shoulder. She tossed it back and gave her head a small shake and returned to her work.

'Good,' the teacher observed and straightened up to look around at the others. 'Does anyone need anything?' He held up a pair of scissors. 'Here's a pair of scissors if anyone is doing any cutting out.'

He moved along the edge of the sky, slowed, and pointed. 'A little yellow,' he suggested. 'You want it? Don't you want it?' He shrugged amiably and went further to watch another girl hard at work. 'How is it coming?' He grinned broadly and pointed as two children leaned over to observe their friend's work. 'Look, look at that.'

Joe started across the blue paper, to a place where he thought he wouldn't be in the way, when a girl's voice cried out in Italian, 'He stepped on my star with his foot.'

Joe looked down and saw what had happened and, embarrassed, backed off. 'I'm sorry.'

The teacher looked up and saw Joe. Joe turned and their eyes met as a little boy's voice said accusingly, 'It's him, teacher.'

The teacher stared another moment, and then indicated Joe's feet. 'Your shoes,' he said in Italian, and repeated it. 'Your shoes. Look, put them over there, with the other ones.'

He turned away and looked at another section of the sky. 'Let's see how this planetarium is coming, let's take a look.'

Joe took his shoes off carefully and went over and set them along the wall with all of the other pairs. 'Something's missing, huh?' the teacher was saying, and then Joe heard him addressing him. 'Listen, pedestrian,' he said in Italian, and all the kids laughed. Joe looked up and saw the man looking at him. 'There, in front of you, fill in that space.' He pointed to the area on the paper he was referring to. 'In front of you.'

Joe didn't move. He felt self-conscious about being barefoot in the middle of all those kids. The teacher came over with some chalk and handed it to him and pointed to the area he was referring to. 'Right there,' he said.

Joe got down on hands and knees, and started to work. Around him, the kids were chattering as they worked. Some of the girls started to chant a little rhyming song, a few clapping their hands with the melody. The teacher moved among them. 'Good,' he commented in Italian. 'Yes, yes. Tell me, tell me,' he was saying in one corner of the room, and then from another corner Joe heard, 'Look, do you like that? Do you like the blue?'

' – There . . .'

' – I understand . . .'

' – Don't break the boxes . . .'

' – Let's go, let's go!'

Joe didn't realize parents had started to come into the room, and continued to work. He heard the teacher's voice greeting people in Italian, but still didn't look up. 'Good day, Madame. This way, please. Open the door. Good day, good day. How are you? Good day . . .'

It was when parents were returning the greeting – '*Buongiorno, buongiorno, buongiorno* – ' that Joe finally looked up from his work. All of the children had finished their work and were standing around him, looking down at what he'd drawn.

Joe looked back at the paper. He had drawn a large glowing moon, detailed and magical. He looked around again, and realized parents had filled the room, standing against the walls not to hurt the 'planetarium'. Joe stared from one to the other, at the faces of shopkeepers and office workers, their expressions concerned and worn, and gently amused. Joe got up and absently wiped his knees with both hands, and stepped back from his work.

The teacher gave him a brief look, and then addressed the parents. 'This,' he began in Italian and spread his hands, 'is our planetarium. Let's take a look and see how it's come out. Be careful where you step so you don't ruin it. Careful!'

The parents took gingerly steps out on to the paper and peered, and quickly stepped off of it to return to their places along the wall.

'Today,' the teacher went on when he had everyone's attention, 'is the last day of school. When you all come back from your vacations you will find your sky stuck up above you, as a memory of your imaginations. You've all done so very well.

'Bye, to you all. Have a wonderful vacation.'

The parents began helping their children collect their things as the children pulled on their shoes. There was total confusion but it lasted only a moment, and then the room was completely quiet and the teacher was left by himself. He went over to where he had left his own shoes. There was only one pair left there against the wall, but they weren't his. They were Joe's.

The teacher considered them a moment, and then picked them up and laboriously pulled them on. Much to his surprise, they were not an impossible fit. He put the few remaining papers and books into his briefcase, slipped on his jacket, put on his hat, and walked out of the classroom. The porter was at the school's main door, and when the teacher passed him he gave a small wave and said, '*Buona vacanza*, Cesare.'

Cesare nodded in return and said in Italian, 'The same to you, sir.'

He closed the gate behind the teacher and locked it. The teacher looked around, as if expecting someone to be there, and then set off swinging his briefcase. When he was a short way down the street, Joe stepped out of a doorway, and followed.

Joe followed his father all the way to a small bus stop. He stayed about thirty feet behind him, and when his father stopped to buy a paper, Joe stopped and ducked behind a vendor's cart. He saw his father leaf through a few magazines and then pick out one and pay for it. When he headed for the station, Joe stepped out from concealment and hurried after him. He stopped at the newspaper stand and bought a copy of the same magazine. Then he followed his father into the shadow of the bus platform.

On the platform, a bus had stopped and its doors were open. Joe spotted his father climbing in and climbed on. He made sure his father had taken a seat and then moved to where he found a seat between an old woman and a *Carabinere*. He took out his magazine and opened it and began to stare at the pages. A few moments later the bus shook and then started off.

They came out into the country very quickly, after passing

through cramped and crowded neighbourhoods. Joe looked up from time to time, to observe his father.

The teacher sat with his feet up on the seat across from him. He was looking at his copy of the magazine. He stopped to read a page.

Joe craned his neck to see which page his father was reading, and then turned to the same page in his own copy of the magazine. It was a story about the poet who had been murdered.

There were photographs of the man as a child and then as a young student. Two of his first published poems were reprinted, but Joe had no way of knowing what they were about.

When the bus started to slow down he looked up and saw his father turning over more pages of the magazine. Joe hurriedly turned pages, as if to keep up, and when he looked up, the bus had stopped and his father was gone. Joe jumped to his feet and hopped out just in time.

He found himself in the countryside. The platform on which he stood was white, as if its concrete had somehow been bleached white. There were oleanders growing along one side, with tall eucalyptus trees throwing a bit of shade. Joe could smell the sea somewhere nearby, and looked around. He saw his father in the distance, walking down the road, his pace measured, comfortable, the walk of a man on his way home.

Joe set out after him, keeping as best he could to the side of the road where trees grew. They passed several girls on bicycles. They were tanned and lean and laughed merrily as they passed, one of them turning her head to give Joe a look, as if she had somehow connected him to the man walking along up ahead. She wore a bikini bathing suit and Joe wondered if she and her friends were on their way to go swimming or had just come from swimming.

He kept a few hundred feet behind his father, moving along the road cautiously. It ran straight as an arrow, built on a strip of land which separated a small inland lake from the sea itself. The road continued until it ended against a small hill. There were sand dunes there, between the road and the sea, and beyond the dunes villas could be seen, almost hidden. Joe's father stopped and took off Joe's shoes, and continued barefoot, the shoes in his hand. He went along to the gate of a small villa and turned in. Joe stopped, and then found a small path leading down to the beach, and turned into it.

He came running down from the slope of the dune and burst out into the open beach. The water was there before him. Further up the beach he could see a few people in the sea. Joe stopped and searched for the house where his father had turned in. There were a few villas backing on to the sea. He wasn't sure which one was his father's.

It was when he had advanced about fifty feet and saw the nearest villa that his heart gave a jump and he stopped in his tracks. For some reason, he was sure he knew where he was. He took a deep breath, fighting down sudden panic, and started to race up the nearest sand dune.

When he came over the top he spotted the veranda running along the white house. He dropped to the sand and hid himself from view as he watched his father come out from inside the house. There was a woman on the veranda, sitting in a big chair, knitting. A beach umbrella had been set up to keep the sun off of her.

When Joe's father came out he was without his jacket and now Joe watched him methodically begin to roll up his shirt sleeves. The woman looked up and he said something to her which made her smile. Then he leaned over and gave her a small kiss on the cheek. She said something to him, and he nodded and went back into the house.

Joe inched down one side of the dune, hoping the woman would not look up from her knitting. He moved forward until he found himself below the veranda. The dune rose before him leading up from the beach to the level of the house. He felt tight in the chest and breathing came hard. He heard footsteps on the veranda and stopped breathing completely. 'He drew this moon with three eyes, two noses, and a mouth,' he heard his father saying in Italian. Joe understood the word for moon, '*luna*', and knew he was talking about Joe's drawing.

'And he stole your shoes,' the woman answered in Italian.

'Why do you have to say stole, please,' the man said in Italian. 'Maybe he made a mistake. After all, we wear the same size.'

Joe hesitated, and then tossed his father's shoes over the railing on to the veranda, and himself followed. His father was holding a small plate in his hand There was an apple on it, and a small knife, and his father had pulled a chair over preparing to sit down and peel the apple for himself.

'I brought your shoes back,' Joe said.

His father smiled and rose. 'I'll go get yours,' he said in Italian. 'Wait,' and in English added, 'I go and get yours.' He turned and went into the house.

Joe stood shifting from one foot to the other, feeling the woman's eyes on him. She was old, older than his father, with soft eyes and greying hair. 'Do you want something to drink?' she asked him in Italian. She mimed holding a glass in her hand and raised it to suggest drinking.

'No thank you,' Joe answered, burning with curiosity.

'Are you English,' she asked him with a strong accent.

'American,' Joe answered as his father reappeared, Joe's shoes in his hand.

'Here they are,' he said in Italian, but hesitated handing them over. He looked at his own shoes in Joe's hand. 'Do you prefer my shoes?' he asked in English.

Instead of answering the question, Joe said, 'You used to speak English a lot, didn't you?'

The man smiled and gave a small shake of his head. 'No, I forgot.' His accent was strong, but he pronounced the words with precision. 'Many years ago,' he went on, 'I knew certain American songs, and things.'

'Do you remember you had a son?' Joe said.

The older woman looked from Joe to his father, and stuck her knitting into its basket. 'I'll play something for you,' she said, and rose with dignity.

'*Grazie, Mamma,*' Joe's father said, as she walked by, trailing some yarn which had caught on her beach gown.

Joe found himself staring at the length of yarn. Something

in him was being pulled, but he didn't know where it came from, or what it was. He heard the music from the piano start, and looked back at his father, who seemed calm, genial. 'He never forgot you,' Joe said, swallowing hard. 'He looked for you everywhere. All he wanted to do was find you. It drove him crazy.' His father listened, impassively, eyes direct, watching him carefully.

'After a while he started shooting up,' Joe continued. 'H! Heroin, you know? We'd shoot up together and then we'd go look for you.'

'Shoot?' his father said, as if he'd not understood the word.

Joe nodded, anger flooding through him. 'Right. You don't believe me, huh?' He turned his arm to show him the inside of the joint, at the elbow, the pocked vein. 'Look! Look! Look at it.'

The piano stopped playing, but neither Joe nor his father noticed. His father stared at Joe's ravaged arm and then looked up into Joe's pale face. 'Where is he?' he demanded.

'He's dead,' Joe said, and couldn't help himself and started to cry. 'He died in front of my house. He OD'd. Overdose.'

His father came over abruptly and held out Joe's shoes. 'Here,' he said with quiet tension and pain. 'Get out. Please . . .'

'Where is Caterina?' his mother said.

Joe turned and saw her standing in the doorway. He wiped his eyes, but more tears came. 'She's rehearsing,' he said bitterly, turned, and ran off the veranda on to the dune, towards the beach.

His father stared after him, and then sagged. 'Mamma,' he said unhappily. 'Mamma.' He turned, and went over to where Joe had thrown the other pair of shoes.

TWELVE

The rehearsal had been going on all afternoon, and everyone was feeling ragged. By the end of the afternoon, as the sky began to change colours and the setting sun was throwing out a fan of deep scarlets, the conductor was determined to get through the last scene of the third act and be certain everyone had it right.

The last scene of *The Masked Ball* is the ball itself. It takes place in an enormous ballroom, and the guests are masked. As Joe came around and began up the ramp leading to the gigantic stage of Caracalla, the theatre space created out of the old Roman baths, he could hear the music begin. He came up to stage level as a throng of dancers tripped merrily across the stage, followed by members of the chorus, also dressed as guests, singing about the love and dances filling the happy ballroom.

Joe moved through the dancers and singers, looking for Caterina. He came to one side of the set as the opening moment of the scene ended and the director called for a halt. The conductor started discussing something with the members of the orchestra, set up to one side on the stage, while the stage manager rushed over and began rearranging several of the characters. 'Stefano, Renato, Francesco, what did I tell you before,' he cried in Italian. 'You die here. That's what we said before.' Joe was nearby and the stage manager was shifting people over and almost tripped over Joe.

'Excuse me,' he said irritably, 'what are you doing here?' He spoke in Italian, but Joe had a good idea what he was talking about. 'Have some consideration, please. Go!' he added more sharply, and Joe moved quickly off to one side as the man turned back to his chorus and dancers. 'Let's go,' he ordered. 'Remember your marks from before.'

Joe found an empty chair among the abandoned orchestra seats, and sat down. He didn't hear the stage director call for everyone to start over, and only when a musician tapped him on the shoulder and said, 'Sorry,' and indicated Joe was in his chair, did he understand he was still in everyone's way. He got up, and wandered across towards the wings, trying to find Caterina.

The music resumed, and he saw Marina, leaning against a flat, watching the rehearsal. 'Where's my mother?' he said when he came up to her.

Marina's eyes were on the stage, and she answered, as if Joe was playing Renato, the betrayed husband of the opera who is trying to identify his wife's lover at this masked ball, '*So you want to know what he is wearing?*'

'Where is she?' Joe repeated.

'Guess,' Marina said.

Joe turned back and watched as the conductor tapped his podium for silence and the bustle ceased and everyone's attention was directed to him. 'From Renato's cue,' he instructed in Italian, 'to Oscar for his song.'

The music began, the strong Verdian melodics, and Renato sang: '*Come, calm yourself, at least tell me something about his costume.*'

It went on like this through the opening of the scene. Joe followed as best he could. There were more stops and starts. The prompter shouted cues, the conductor had the orchestra start from the previous measure. And then the conductor was saying, 'Riccardo, Amelia, from "*invan ti celi, Amelia*".'

The music began again. Riccardo, the man in love with Amelia, Renato's wife, did not know there was a plot to murder him. He was masked, as was Amelia. They have recognized one another. She has tried to warn him, insisting she cannot identify herself to him. But he knows her, and sings: '*In vain, in vain you hide, Amelia, the angel, it is you!*'

'*I love you, yes, I love you,*' the character of Amelia spoke rather than sang, and Joe recognized his mother. '. . . *and I prostrate myself at your feet in tears.'* She turned, and began to cross the stage slowly, in Joe's direction. ' – *Tomorrow you'll be a corpse if you stay,'* she said. There was something forced in her delivery and she seemed very uncomfortable. '*Save yourself. Go. Leave me. Flee, flee.'* She came up to where Joe stood with Marina, and over her shoulder called out, 'Five minutes. Five minutes, please. Five minutes, please.' Without waiting for an answer, she took Joe under the arm, and walked with him offstage.

Everyone immediately broke from their positions. A small truck with coffee and refreshments put-putted on to the stage and the dancers and chorus hurried over to it and began shouting orders. Edward hopped off the back of the truck with surprising agility and came over to Marina.

'You got a job, Edward,' she said.

'They wouldn't allow me in here,' he said. 'I knew that Caterina didn't want me to miss her *Ballo.*' He took a big book out from under his arm and opened it to show Marina. 'Look what an incredible present I found for her; the score of *Ballo* autographed by Callas. Isn't that extraordinary?'

'Caterina is beyond all that now,' Marina said. She turned, and started in the direction Caterina had taken.

Edward slowed to look around at the overwhelming theatre, and then followed. 'Yes,' he said, 'I suppose this is a tricky place. How is she singing?'

'She's not singing,' Marina said. 'She's speaking her role.'

'That's very unusual for her,' Edward said, thoughtful and polite.

Marina stopped before a door which led beneath the big stage and fixed him with a look bordering on resentment. 'You don't understand anything,' she said.

Edward followed Marina out of the bright light into the dim stairwell. It took him some moments for his eyes to get accustomed to the dark. 'I love her voice,' he said.

'I love her,' he heard Marina answer.

'Oh, bullshit,' Edward said and walked down several steps

until he noticed that Marina had stopped. 'Really,' he went on, mildly scandalized and annoyed with her. 'That's completely missing the point. Who can tell the dancer from the dance?'

'I love her,' Marina said, and Edward saw she was staring off into the ill-lit gloom. 'I love her.'

Caterina had her arms around Joe. They were both crying. Neither Edward nor Marina could hear what they were saying, but they saw the look of comfort in Caterina's face as she gazed at her son.

'Now you're in love with your father,' she was saying to Joe.

'You really screwed me up, you know,' he said. 'I'm half Italian.'

Neither of them noticed Marina and Edward watching from nearby.

'You're American,' Caterina said and laughed. 'You were born in New York. Your father is Douglas Winter. It says so on your birth certificate.'

'You could go to jail for forging my birth certificate,' Joe said.

'They'd never arrest me,' Caterina declared playfully. 'I'm pregnant.'

Joe pulled away and said, 'No kidding?' with innocent surprise.

Caterina burst out laughing. 'Oh, honey,' she said and caressed her face, 'I'm teasing, darling. I'm sorry. I'm sorry.' She reached out and wiped his tear-streaked face with the corner of her costume. 'Here . . .'

Edward and Marina turned, and quietly went back up to the stage.

'Why did you break up?' Joe asked Caterina.

'He hated my voice,' she said, and paused. She grew momentarily thoughtful, remembering. 'He wanted something different. He was selfish. We weren't right for each other. She looked at her son, and added, 'He was in love with his mother.'

Joe coughed, almost gagging, and pretended to be sneezing to cover his momentary sense of shock.

From above them a man's voice called out, '*A posto. La pausa e finita. A posto, signori.*'

'The break's over,' Caterina said. 'I have to get back on stage.'

'Positions, please,' someone else was shouting. 'Positions.'

'I have to go,' she said to Joe and gave him one last hug and then turned and led him back to the stairs.

Joe went and took a seat in the front of the theatre as Caterina resumed her place on stage. 'People in place,' the assistant director was crying, 'the break is over!'

Joe saw the figure of his father, Giuseppe, appear at the back of the stage and move carefully through the chorus members until he was right behind Caterina. She was waiting for her cue when she turned, as if some instinct had signalled her, and saw him.

Giuseppe took both her hands in his and stared at her, his expression sad. 'It's terrible, no?' he said in Italian.

'Terrible?' she answered, her emotions confused, 'to see me once more is terrible?'

'Is it true?' he went on in Italian.

'What?' she asked.

'Our son . . .' He gazed at her, and tenderly took her in his arms.

From where he sat, Joe stared at that sight on the stage. Now, finally, some image which had been lost to him, came back to life and was once more real. His mother and his father stood rejoined into a single figure. They separated once more and said something to each other Joe couldn't hear. But it didn't matter, and he began to applaud.

All eyes went to him, sitting by himself.

Giuseppe made his way across the stage to a flight of stairs leading down to the audience. He walked slowly across a row, until he was not too far from Joe. When he was close to him, he cried, 'Hey!'

Joe started to get to his feet, apprehension boiling inside him. He was shaking from excitement and fear. 'Yes?'

Seconds later, his father stood in front of him. 'So,' he said, and his hand went back and he swung and struck Joe across the face.

Joe staggered, but didn't fall. He caught himself and stood, sparks flying in his head, eyes dancing. When he could see clearly, Giuseppe had moved to sit down several rows in front of him. Joe stared at him, and then looked up at the stage, at Caterina.

She had seen Giuseppe strike his son, and now watched the two figures even as the music continued and she, as Amelia, played out her final moments with Riccardo, who was about to be slain by Amelia's jealous husband. Joe's eyes glowed with a curious joy, and he stared up at her as she sang: '*I love you, yes, I love you . . .*' The words were meant for her doomed lover, Riccardo, but she addressed them to the two figures sitting in the audience.

Giuseppe raised his head and stared up at Caterina, and then turned and looked back at his son. Joe met his gaze, and smiled. A terrible sense of despair came over Giuseppe, and he buried his face in his hands. Beyond him, on the stage, Riccardo was singing: '*As long as you love me, Amelia, I care not for my fate.*'

Marina sat to one side, Edward near her. He was following the music with the score, glancing up from time to time to absorb the action, but returning almost immediately to the compelling power of Verdi's music as he traced it on the pages before him. Marina's eyes were only on Caterina. She saw the exchanges taking place from stage to audience, and saw Joe and Giuseppe looking at one another, and then back up at Caterina.

'Flee!' Amelia was pleading with Riccardo. '*Save yourself.*'

'Joe,' a voice said, and he turned. Ariana was behind him, bending over to touch him on the shoulder as she spoke. 'Mustafa wanted to find you.'

Joe barely nodded, and turned his attention back to the stage.

'I wish you to be saved!' Riccardo was singing.

'He's leaving,' Ariana said. 'He didn't know where to look for you.' She realized Joe wasn't listening, that he was looking only up at the stage, or over at the man bent in his seat, his head in his hands. 'He wanted to say goodbye.'

Giuseppe looked up slowly. Caterina was gazing straight at him, as Riccardo sang to her, *'My heart is breaking . . .'* Giuseppe turned, and saw Joe. The boy smiled at him once more. This time, Giuseppe returned it.

Caterina saw the two exchange looks, and then Riccardo was bidding her a final farewell. *'For the last time,'* he sang, *'goodbye.'*

'Goodbye,' Caterina responded, and turned to address Riccardo as he clasped her hands. *'Goodbye.'*

Frank de Felitta
The Entity £1.25

Carlotta Moran, a widow with three children, still young and attractive enough to build a new life – until something hideous enters her world. To the psychiatrists she is deranged, a hysteric on the brink of schizophrenia – to the psychic researchers her experiences are beyond the credibility of science . . . Night after night a formless malevolence possesses her – a sexual scavenger from the outer reaches of the unknown . . .

The ultimate novel of supernatural terror and sexual horror.

John Ives
Fear 95p

When the crazy Navaho, Calvin Duggai, made his break for freedom he was driven by hate that burned like the desert sun. Out of the world of echoing corridors where the white man imprisons the criminally insane to seek out the four doctors who certified him. To take them into the burning desert of Arizona, to strip them naked and watch them die in the sun-blistered wilderness of sand and scorpion . . .

You can buy these and other Pan Books from booksellers and newsagents; or direct from the following address:
Pan Books, Sales Office, Cavaye Place, London SW10 9PG
Send purchase price plus 20p for the first book and 10p for each additional book, to allow for postage and packing
Prices quoted are applicable in the UK

While every effort is made to keep prices low, it is sometimes necessary to increase prices at short notice. Pan Books reserve the right to show on covers and charge new retail prices which may differ from those advertised in the text or elsewhere